SEP 0 3

DATE DUE

NO 23 '03			
MR 04 '04			
4-28-0			
6-22-04			
JUL 11 '05			
9-28-			
12-6-			
2-6-08			
3-6-0			
JUL 02 '08			
12-4-14			
GAYLORD			PRINTED IN U.S.A.

Scent of Heather

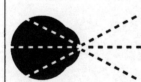

This Large Print Book carries the
Seal of Approval of N.A.V.H.

Scent of Heather

Jane Peart

Thorndike Press • Waterville, Maine

Published in 2003 by arrangement with
Natasha Kern Literary Agency, Inc.

Thorndike Press® Large Print Christian Fiction Series.

The tree indicium is a trademark of Thorndike Press.

The text of this Large Print edition is unabridged.
Other aspects of the book may vary from the original edition.

Set in 16 pt. Plantin.

Printed in the United States on permanent paper.

Library of Congress Cataloging-in-Publication Data

Peart, Jane.
    Scent of heather / Jane Peart.
        p. cm.
    ISBN 0-7862-4650-2 (lg. print : hc : alk. paper)
    1. Americans — Great Britain — Fiction.   2. Large type
books.   I. Title.
PS3566.E238 S28 2003
    813′.54—dc21   2002190714

Scent of Heather

As the Founder/CEO of NAVH, the only national health agency solely devoted to those who, although not totally blind, have an eye disease which could lead to serious visual impairment, I am pleased to recognize Thorndike Press★ as one of the leading publishers in the large print field.

Founded in 1954 in San Francisco to prepare large print textbooks for partially seeing children, NAVH became the pioneer and standard setting agency in the preparation of large type.

Today, those publishers who meet our standards carry the prestigious "Seal of Approval" indicating high quality large print. We are delighted that Thorndike Press is one of the publishers whose titles meet these standards. We are also pleased to recognize the significant contribution Thorndike Press is making in this important and growing field.

Lorraine H. Marchi, L.H.D.
Founder/CEO
NAVH

★ Thorndike Press encompasses the following imprints: Thorndike, Wheeler, Walker and Large Pr int Press.

Chapter One

Jess had not the slightest premonition when she first spotted the elegant young Englishman in well-cut tweeds walking confidently through London's crowded Heathrow Airport. As he approached the passenger lounge where she waited with the small group of American tourists just off the plane from New York, she thought to herself. *He's handsome enough to be in the movies or on television.*

With a trim, athletic build, classic features, and smooth hair the color of polished maple, he certainly could have been. However, something indefinable about him arrested her attention more than his obvious good looks. Maybe it was his air of easy assurance, the aristocratic bearing that only a background of wealth and privilege can bestow.

Whatever it was, Jess could not have been more surprised when he stepped up to the group and announced, "Hello, everyone. I'm Peter Fortnay, Colonel Fortnay's nephew."

She listened in astonished delight as he proceeded to tell them in a clear, upper-class British accent, "My apologies for not being here the minute you stepped from the plane. Incredible traffic this time of day and I'm sorry to be late. I've come in place of Uncle Alec." *He smiled as if this were a calamity instead of a pleasant surprise,* Jess thought.

Of course, lately, her life had been full of pleasant surprises. The biggest, most wonderful one had been Aunt Mil's invitation to be her traveling companion on this trip to England she had won as a prize in the TV Trivia contest.

"I'm afraid I have some rather bad news," Peter went on. "My uncle took a nasty spill last weekend while he was trying out a new horse he's been training, and he'll be laid up for a few weeks with a wrenched back."

There was a murmur of sympathy all around before someone demanded, "But what about our tour?"

Half boyish shyness but all charm, Peter Fortnay smiled and said diffidently, "I'm going to take Uncle's place as your tour guide until he's up and about again. I'm a

8

rather poor substitute as a tour guide, not having his experience and knowledge, but perhaps you'll put up with me for a short time."

Not a poor substitute at all, Jess thought with inner amusement as she caught Aunt Mil's sly wink. Only hours ago on the plane, her aunt had expressed some concern that Jess, at twenty-three, was the only member of the tour under thirty. With the arrival of Peter Fortnay, things were decidedly looking up!

Peter continued, "There'll be some others joining us. They've come in on other airlines and are going through customs now getting their passports cleared. It shouldn't take long. Then we'll be off. I know all of you must be tired after the long flight, and I regret the delay. We'll make it up to you, I assure you, if you'll just bear with it a bit longer."

Peter looked around engagingly. His eyes, a lighter brown than his hair and darkly lashed, lingered for a moment on Jess. She felt her cheeks grow warm under his interested gaze and was happy she'd had her naturally curly hair smartly styled short just before she left on the trip. She was also glad her blazer, sweater, and skirt were nicely mixed shades of blue, her most flattering color.

Jess could not know that Peter was not paying any particular attention to the becoming gamin hairstyle or the outfit. But he was noticing a slim, pretty girl with glossy dark hair, amazing blue-green eyes, a straight little nose lightly sprinkled with golden freckles, and a sweetly curved mouth.

Then he went on talking. "We'll be traveling in two minibuses. So we may as well get your group settled now and fill up the second bus with the latecomers. If you'll just follow me. . . ."

Anywhere! Lead on! Jess thought, wishing her friend Pam, who had predicted she would find romance on this trip, could see Peter Fortnay, a man straight out of any woman's dream! His presence completed her sensation that on this trip she was living a dream come true.

At the luggage claim area, Jess collected her tote bag and carry-on case. As she walked through the crowded terminal, Jess finally began to assimilate the fact that she was actually in *England.* While others might dream of traveling to Venice, Florence, Rome, or Paris, for Jess it had always been England she longed to see. And Scotland too, because it was the homeland of her Grandmother Jeanie as well as the ancestral heritage of all her family.

Jess glanced affectionately at her aunt. If it had not been for the cleverness of this canny Scotswoman, she would never have had this once-in-a-lifetime chance. Millicent Macdonald — with her graying red hair, snapping blue eyes behind glasses, energetic personality, and wiry build — was a most unlikely looking fairy godmother. But she had certainly made Jessamyn's abiding wish come true by winning the contest.

While the rest of their luggage was being loaded into the storage compartment of a gleaming minibus, Peter was standing at the door helping people aboard.

The eight Americans who had assembled at Kennedy Airport in New York early that morning had quickly become a congenial group. Besides Aunt Mil and herself, there was Emily Mason, a vivacious widow on her first trip to Europe, and also Don and Yvonne Trench, a breezy, outgoing ranching couple from Texas who told everyone jokingly that they were spending their children's inheritance. From the look of the diamonds they both wore, their tooled leather boots, and Yvonne's mink jacket, Jess gathered that even after this trip there would be plenty left for children and grandchildren.

Another couple, the Coopleys, were celebrating their fortieth anniversary by taking a second honeymoon. They were a quiet, silver-haired pair who looked more like brother and sister than husband and wife. Patricia Hollings completed the party that had flown with the group from the States. She had informed them immediately that as the executive secretary for an international lawyer she was widely traveled and had made many trips abroad. Jess knew instinctively that Ms. Hollings would be very vocal and could possibly become a bore.

However, Jess was too thrilled about the tour to let anything or anyone disturb her happiness. She meant to enjoy every minute.

Just as she was about to get on the bus, Jess became aware of a commotion of some sort — raised voices and the sound of argument. She turned to see a porter in an excited exchange with the driver of their minibus. She could not understand a word of the pure Cockney accent but Peter stepped in at once. Sure that if anyone could get a handle on the confusion Peter could, Jess got on the bus.

Whether by accident or design, Aunt Mil had seated herself with Emily Mason, and the double seat just behind the driver was empty. Casting a discreet glance at her aunt who looked totally innocent, Jess had a sneaking suspicion that Aunt Mil was hoping Peter Fortnay would take the vacant seat beside Jess when he boarded the bus.

Laughing to herself at her aunt's deviousness, Jess sat down and started looking over the brochures for this unusual tour.

The most unique feature offered was that aside from the days spent in London at the beginning and the end of the tour, they would stay in elegant, historical private country manors as "guests" of the distinguished owners. Jess noted, with new interest and a flurry of excitement, that among these homes would be Fortnay Hall, ancestral home of the Fortnays, "a family descended from the Plantagenets."

The brochure went on to describe in glowing terms what to expect. "As we go into the heart of England, far removed from the press of ordinary tours, you will spend leisurely days traveling along quiet leafy lanes; visiting historic sites; roaming along the cliffs and the high, deserted moors; passing through the legendary Sherwood Forest; touring Stratford-upon-Avon, Shakespeare's birthplace; attending two of his plays at the magnificent new theater; driving to the cobbled Yorkshire town of Haworth, known as Brontë country; and exploring a medieval castle. Each evening you will return to the comfort of one of the great homes to dine by candlelight and enjoy traditional English hospitality."

It sounds like something you'd read about, Jess thought with a delicious sense of anticipation thrilling all through her. Something that happens to someone else. *But it's happening to me!* she reminded herself enthusiastically.

Afterward, Jess was never sure what made her look up and glance out the window at exactly that moment. As she did she saw a tall man coming out of the terminal entrance. He stood there, looking about, towering above the other people milling out the door. He had slung his raincoat over one broad shoulder, a camera case and haversack over the other. He was six feet of rangy height, with tousled russet-red hair. His strong-featured face might have been ruggedly handsome if he had not been scowling.

Suddenly his sweeping glance caught Jess's and for a fraction of a second their eyes locked. The impact was immediate. It was so unexpected, like a flash of summer lightning, it momentarily stunned her. Quickly she turned away, not knowing what to make of her strange sensation — a kind of

14

innate recognition — as elusive as it was real.

Just then Peter, stepping into the bus, stood at the doorway and made another announcement. "Sorry, everyone, there'll be a little more delay. It seems there's to be a last-minute change. Another tour overbooked and left someone without a place. So he'll be coming with us. We're taking care of his baggage now and we'll be under way in a few minutes. I do appreciate your patience," he said with that devastating smile.

Good-natured moans and half-hearted laughter erupted throughout the bus. "We'll probably never hear the end of the stupid travel agent who left the guy stranded!" groaned Don Trench.

"Let's hope not. There's nothing worse than a complaining bore on a tour," agreed Patricia Hollings, with the air of one who has been in such a situation before.

"I can't imagine a travel agency making such a mistake," Emily Mason gently commented.

"That's because you haven't traveled much," Ms. Hollings replied authoritatively.

"Keep your fingers crossed that he's a good sport," Yvonne suggested.

Jess sighed and settled back to reading the brochures. She had not slept much on the plane and was now feeling tired and a little stiff from all that sitting. Excitement was combined with the change of time to make her feel slightly dazed. It would be good to get to the hotel, have a hot bath, sleep for a while, then start exploring the fabulous city of London. It sounded so wonderful.

Looking out the window she saw Peter marshaling the newly arrived members of the tour onto the second minibus. Aunt Mil had received a list of those taking this tour that told their names and where they were from. Now Jess occupied herself with trying to decide who was who.

She guessed the plump, rosy-cheeked couple must be the Baults, from Belgium. They were chatting animatedly with a powerfully built dark-eyed man with a marvelous head of steel gray curls who must be Dr. Stavros from Greece. There were two more — a scholarly middle-aged man and an attractive, stylishly dressed woman. That made five members of that group. She noticed that she was still the youngest member of the tour.

Expecting that Peter would get the other group settled, then fill the unoccupied seat beside her so that they'd soon be under way, Jess was startled when a deep, masculine, totally American voice asked, "May I?"

16

She turned and looked directly up into keen blue eyes in a lean, intelligent face. She suppressed an instinctive gasp. It was the red-haired man with whom she had had that strange unsettling eye contact!

"You weren't saving this for anyone, then?" he demanded, frowning. An edge of irritation entered his voice at her hesitation.

"No," Jess murmured, then turned quickly to stare out the window, annoyingly aware of her quickened heartbeat.

"All set, everyone?" the jovial voice of their driver rang out, and Jess felt a small stab of disappointment as she realized Peter must have gone with the new group in the other minibus. Oh, well, she would probably see a lot of Peter Fortnay on the tour. As the bus began to pull out through the heavy airport traffic, she cheerfully leaned forward to peer eagerly out the window.

Her first impression of London was misty with fog. Even so it was almost overwhelming. The minibus spun along the expressway, matching the excessive speed of the dizzying traffic. Blocks of buildings flashed by. Jess found herself dismayed by rushing billboards, overpasses, and cars pouring in from approach roads. *This* wasn't the London of her dreams!

As if echoing her thoughts, the man beside her said gruffly, "It's even worse than when I was here four years ago. England seems bent on destroying itself. These expressways, row houses, blocks of cement passing for architecture — soon there'll be nothing left of this magnificent city. The whole country is going down the tubes —"

Immediately Jess resented his disparaging remark and spontaneously flew to the defense of *her* London.

"But, of course, the expressway is the worst part in any big city," Jess replied, still determinedly cheerful. "And we'll be seeing the other parts, the real England, on this tour."

His eyes were coldly appraising, like blue ice, as he regarded Jess, then said with an edge of sarcasm, "I suppose you were duped into taking this romanticized package tour to the 'heartland of England'?"

Jess shot him a quick look, thinking perhaps he was kidding. But she saw no laughter in those snapping blue eyes.

Bristling indignantly at his sarcastic attitude, she said coolly, "I don't believe I'd say I was duped. In fact, I think it all sounds great!"

"It's all super-hype, you know. A part of the unreal image projected to unsuspecting

18

tourists." He paused. "But maybe you're one of those incurable romantics who go for this sort of thing."

"I don't like labels," Jess said sharply. "What do you mean — 'a romantic'?"

"Well, anyone would have to be a romantic to be misled by all this nonsense in this brochure." He thumped the folded one he held, identical to the one Jess had pored over excitedly for weeks and had just happily re-read.

Checking a sharp retort, Jess swallowed hard instead and turned to look out the window again. Inside, she determined that she would make a point of steering clear of this fellow from now on. She certainly wasn't going to allow him to ruin this trip for her.

In a moment he broke into the stony silence that had followed his last comment, saying, "Look, I'm sorry if I was out of line. And I apologize. I agree with you about labels. So I hope you won't label *me* a skeptic!"

Reluctantly Jess turned her head. Now there seemed to be a hint of laughter in those penetrating blue eyes.

"I guess I'm off kilter. My plane from California was four hours late getting into New York. I had to run for my London flight. Then when I got here the whole tour thing fell apart!" he paused and said appealingly, "I hope you'll put my bad temper down to jet lag or something."

A suggestion of a smile tugged at his firm mouth as he thrust out his hand toward her. "I'm Graham Campbell."

With only a slight hesitation, Jess offered her hand and at once felt it enclosed by his large, solid grip. "Jessamyn Baird," she said in a low voice.

"Jessamyn," he repeated. "Lovely name. Scottish, isn't it?" He smiled broadly then. "Lovely and *romantic*. For all their bad press the Scots *are* very romantic, you know. Whether you like labels or not, it's true."

There was no time for any more conversation because the minibus was pulling up in front of a large timbered Tudor mansion, the elegant townhouse now converted into a small luxury hotel where the group would be staying in London.

Aunt Mil was coming down the aisle as Graham stood up to let Jess pass. Jess started to introduce them but didn't have a chance because her aunt, in her usual forthright manner, held out her hand to him and introduced herself. "Millicent Macdonald," she said pleasantly. "I see you're joining our group."

Graham nodded, smiled, and shook her

hand, saying, "Graham Campbell."

"Campbell," Aunt Mil said briskly, her head tilted to one side. She let her eyes survey all six feet of him shrewdly, then asked, "You've heard of Glencoe, no doubt? That's where *your* ancestors nearly wiped out *mine* in one of the bloodiest massacres in Scottish history. Did you know that?"

Jess looked quickly at Graham, realizing he could not know Aunt Mil's penchant for facts nor her tendency to be abrupt without meaning to give offense. But Graham looked only momentarily taken aback and replied coolly, "Yes, madam, but since I was not there and do not believe in retroactive guilt, I feel no responsibility for something that took place hundreds of years ago."

For once Aunt Mil seemed at a loss for words. Jess knew she had not expected to be taken so seriously nor rebuffed so sharply. Looking disconcerted, she gave a little lift of her chin, whirled around, and quickly marched toward the exit, leaving Jess with the bewildered Graham Campbell.

He shook his head as if to clear it and grinned. "That's quite a formidable lady! I'm glad *you're* not a Macdonald."

"But, I *am* — on my mother's side." Jess told him archly. "And that 'formidable lady' is my aunt."

Graham struck his forehead in mock anguish. "I *am* starting off on the wrong foot!" he declared dramatically. "Surrounded by the enemy."

"At least, you weren't *ambushed* as *our* ancestors were!" Jess retorted, and with a satisfied smile that the last word was hers, she turned and walked to the door of the bus where Peter Fortnay was standing and smiling. Possibly waiting for *her?*

Chapter
Two

"It's like a dream!" Jess sighed happily, closing her eyes and luxuriating in the fragrant steam wafting upward from the warm, perfumed bubbles in the porcelain tub of the pink-tiled bathroom adjoining the bedroom of their hotel suite.

I feel as if I'm on a magic carpet, she thought. She felt she had been transported from her ordinary life into this one of undreamed luxury.

Of course, for Jess, everything about this trip was magical. The call from Aunt Mil had come on the very day Jess received the pink slip in her paycheck envelope. Danby's, where she worked in the book department, was closing its downtown store. In the accompanying "Letter to Our Employees" the management offered to accept applications for anyone wanting to relocate to one of the branch stores in the suburbs.

But Jessamyn had grown up in the suburbs, and what she liked best about working and living in the city was its access to concerts, theater, and classes at the museum.

That evening when she had gone home to her apartment, feeling a little depressed and worried about getting another job, Aunt Mil had phoned long distance to ask if she would like to come along on this prize trip.

Would she? Jess had practically jumped for joy at the chance! It had confirmed for her one of her Grandmother Jeanie's favorite sayings in any disappointment. "God never closes a door unless He opens a window."

Jess smiled remembering how often that conviction had helped her. More and more as she grew up she appreciated the deep faith her grandmother had instilled in all her grandchildren. Jess didn't know what she would have done without it these last two years living in the city alone, away from family and familiar things. It had made a real difference.

"Thank you, Lord, for Grandmother." Jess whispered a spontaneous little prayer. "And thank you for this wonderful experience."

Jess hoped prayers whispered from a froth of bubbles were as acceptable as those prayed anywhere else. If they were genuine, sincere, and heartfelt, she knew they were.

An hour later, refreshed and radiant, dressed in a nubby-knit coral sweater and a softly flared wool skirt with tiny coral, cream, and blue checks, Jess went downstairs. A high tea was set out in the impressive drawing room where most of the other tour members were already gathered.

Her appetite had been dulled by free plane food and too much excitement, but was immediately restored at the sight of the buffet of attractively presented food. Jess was selecting from the variety of cold sliced meats, English cheeses, and fresh, wholesome breads, just as someone came up beside her and spoke.

"You look positively glowing, Miss Baird."

Jess whirled around to find Peter Fortnay smiling at her with frankly admiring eyes.

"Why thank you! I feel absolutely wonderful," she said.

"Then everything is to your liking — your room, I mean?"

"Oh, it's beautiful!" she said enthusiastically, thinking of the luxurious suite she was sharing with Aunt Mil, the small sitting room with rose velvet Victorian furnishings, the bedroom with twin mahogany poster beds, the rose chintz spreads and satin puffs folded at the foot of each, the trellised-rose wallpaper, and the white marble fireplace.

Up close, Peter Fortnay was even more attractive. His brown eyes were thickly lashed, his skin was flawless, and teeth perfect. "Then you're finding everything on the tour satisfactory?" he asked.

"Oh, *more* than satisfactory!" Jess assured him, hard put to keep a straight face just imagining what her friend Pam would say about this specimen of manhood. She probably would accuse Jess of making him up! Or dreaming him up!

Jess blinked, forcing her attention off how Peter looked and on to what he was asking.

"Is there anything you're particularly interested in seeing, any place you want especially to visit?"

"There are so many things, so many —" Jess began.

"Well, according to the schedule the next two days you'll be in London, more or less on your own. Uncle always says the ladies like a couple of days to shop, pick up anything they may have forgotten to bring, just be free. That way they get a better idea of what they want to do and see when we come back to London at the end of the tour," Peter said. "Our first actual trip will be to Kent to visit Canterbury's magnificent cathedral and to walk on Dover's white cliffs. We'll stay two nights there before going on to Warwickshire."

"That sounds marvelous. By the way, I am rather interested in doing some brass rubbings. Would there be a chance there at the cathedral?"

"I'm not sure. In those big churches I believe you must get permission. But I can find out for you. Are you keen on doing them?"

"Well, it was suggested —" Jess started to say when Yvonne interrupted.

"Peter, come on over here for a sec, please. We need you to settle an argument!" She beckoned him laughingly over to where she and Don were clustered with the Belgian couple, Patricia Hollings, and Dr. Stavros.

"Excuse me," Peter said to Jess, lifting his eyebrow slightly as if to indicate he must play the host.

Left alone for the moment Jess recalled with amusement how her "interest" in brass rubbing was "suggested" to her. On one of her last days at work, Esther Whitley, Danby's head decorator, had walked into the book department and confronted Jess. "I hear you're going to England, Baird," she began.

Esther was a kind of character around Danby's, as well-known for her impeccable

27

taste and talent as for her eccentricities. She always wore tinted glasses and a hat, usually a wide-brimmed one that shadowed her sharp-featured face. She had an air of unimpeachable authority, and when she spoke, people listened!

She had faced Jess and said imperiously, "Of course, you'll want to do some brasses while you're there. There's a Brass Rubbing Center right in London near the Tower where you can pick and choose from many different types. But if you'll be traveling about, you'll be able to find some that are not quite so common, I feel sure. You may have to get permission from the vicars of some of the country churches, where you can find some really rare ones. But they are usually very gracious about it."

"Brasses?" Jess echoed, puzzled.

Esther nodded impatiently. "Yes, yes, my dear girl! They've become very chic, very fashionable as decorating pieces, wall hangings, and the like. If you do enough you can sell them when you come back at quite a nice profit. I'd be interested in seeing any you might do. I have clients who are mad for them."

"But, Mrs. Whitley, I don't know what you mean or how to do any," Jess protested.

"It's very simple. You only need a few

items. A small supply of high rag content paper — you can get that in any art supply store, a heelball —"

"Heelball?" Jess interrupted.

"Yes, it's a wax crayon similar to a boot-blacking wax." Esther went on, "Some masking tape to hold the paper in place, a soft-bristled brush for cleaning the brass plate before you begin, a silk cloth to wipe it smooth when you're done." She paused. "The only other thing you need is elbow grease." Esther allowed herself a light smile.

"I'm sorry, but I don't think — well, I still don't understand exactly what 'brasses' are," Jess said timidly.

Esther looked aghast at Jess's ignorance.

"Why they are memorial engravings embedded in church floors or on raised mounts — effigies of famous or infamous people of the twelfth through the fifteenth and sixteenth centuries. They are mostly, of course, of the upper classes. And they are marvelous records of medieval fashion of Britain. Lords, ladies, knights in full armor, bishops, you'll find all sorts of interesting ones if you're alert and looking. My dear girl, they sell from three hundred dollars for the large ones to fifty and sixty for smaller sizes. You could pay for the entire trip if you did enough of them!" Esther declared.

Jess did not bother to tell her that Aunt Mil was paying for her trip, and she promised Esther she would certainly look into doing some brasses and show her any she had done upon her return.

"You know I'll be at the Smithfield branch then," Esther reminded her. She added with a shudder, "*Suburbia!* I hope I can survive it!" as she walked away.

Remembering that conversation, Jess almost laughed.

"What's so funny? Did you know you were smiling to yourself?"

Jess looked up and saw Graham Campbell by her side.

"I was just thinking of an amusing incident that happened before I left my job," she replied.

"What was your job?" he asked.

"Nothing very important. A clerk in the book section of a department store," Jess shrugged. "But it had its advantages since I love to read. I spent most of my store discount on books — you know, those big gorgeous, full-color picture ones they call 'coffee-table' books."

"I didn't know people actually read them. I thought they were only for show, to impress your dinner guests," Graham said.

"Not for me. I pored over them. Actually,

that's where I got all my 'distorted' ideas about England!" she said teasingly but with a little sprinkle of spice.

"*Touché!*" he laughed. "I deserved that." After a slight pause, Graham said, "Then I was right about you after all. You *are* a romantic. You want things to be as you imagine them, as you want them to be."

"Doesn't everybody?"

"No, some people are very pragmatic, realistic."

"But *you're* on this tour!" she accused. "You didn't have to accept this one as a substitute for the one you originally wanted."

Graham had the grace to look a bit sheepish as he explained, "Why am I on this tour? Would you believe, *fate?*" he grinned mischievously. "Actually, I didn't have much choice. I didn't know about the overbooking until I landed, and the travel agency representative met me and tried to talk his way out of the mess. Since my time in England was limited, I had to take the substitute they offered. This tour." Graham shrugged then asked teasingly, "So what's your excuse?"

"Me? Well, England is the one place I've always wanted to visit. I'll see the places I've read about and never thought I'd have a chance to see. If Aunt Mil hadn't —" She broke off as Graham interrupted.

"So this tour is a dream come true? I might have guessed as much. You have the eyes of a dreamer." He smiled knowingly. "Well, you'll be lucky if the reality doesn't destroy your dream." He paused, then said thoughtfully, "It's no longer the England of Shakespeare or Dickens — the one in those well-done travelogues and dramas on public television you know —" His voice trailed off, then abruptly became hearty.

"I honestly hope everything will come up to your expectations. I suppose my attitude is colored by the reason for my trip. I'm gathering material for a 'critical survey' of English literature of the nineteenth century —"

He halted, and Jess regarded him curiously, waiting for him to go on. When he didn't she asked, "Are you a writer?"

"No, I'm a —"

Before he could finish Peter came up to them and addressed Graham. "Well, Mr. Campbell, I hope your change of tour won't prove too much of a disappointment. You may find this one a nice trade."

"I hope so, too. I plan to make the most of it. As Robert Louis Stevenson observed, 'To travel hopefully is a better thing than to arrive.' At least, sometimes," Graham answered with a wry smile.

"And you, Miss Baird, are you looking forward to getting under way for your first tour of London tomorrow?" Peter asked.

"I can hardly wait," Jess said enthusiastically as much for Graham's benefit as Peter's. She was determined not to let the American's cynicism dampen her own optimism.

He lifted an eyebrow, and after a few more exchanges with Peter about some of the aspects of the tour, Graham moved back to replenish his plate at the tea table. Peter and Jess were left alone.

"I can't tell you what a pleasant surprise it was to find you were a member of this tour," Peter said, gazing at Jess with obvious enjoyment. "When Uncle Alec had his accident and assigned me to take his place as tour guide, I was rather dreading the possibility of having to shepherd a bunch of—" Peter stopped as if catching himself — "At any rate, let's say, it was an agreeable shock to see you!"

Jess laughed merrily. "I must confess you were a surprise, too! I already had a confirmed image of our tour guide, Colonel Fortnay, the way pictures always portray the retired British army officer. Balding, with a bit of a paunch, a walrus-stiff mustache, and even sporting a swagger stick!"

Peter threw back his head and laughed. "A sort of cartoon character 'Colonel Blimp,' eh?"

"Yes, I'm ashamed to admit."

"Wait until you actually meet Uncle Alec. You'll see how wrong you were," Peter told her. "He's actually quite striking looking. Slim, straight as an arrow, rides daily, makes quite a dashing appearance. He's been all over the world as an explorer, led several expeditions into the Himalayas, guided safaris in Africa. Besides all the medals he won while he was in the army and during the war, he's been decorated twice by the Queen for his exploits."

"Promise you won't tell him what I was expecting?" pleaded Jess.

"I promise. Your guilty secret is safe with me," Peter said in a stage whisper. "Fortnay Manor, our family home, will be one of the places you'll be staying on the tour, you know. He's quite proud of it and will be thrilled to show it off. That's the part of tour guiding he likes best, I think."

Then Peter leaned close and said to Jess, "I've got a whole new perspective on being a tour guide. I think it's going to be a great deal of fun."

Jess felt her heart rise and give a little leap at Peter's words. And in his eyes and smile she read a great deal more than his words.

For someone like Jess who loved everything and anything English, London proved a magic city, endlessly compelling. During the two free days there, Aunt Mil, Jess, Mrs. Coopley, Emily Mason, and the lady from Texas first headed for the famous Harrod's Department Store.

"When I shopped at Nieman-Marcus in Dallas, I thought I'd seen everything, but this beats all!" Yvonne Trench drawled.

It beats Danby's, too, Jess thought as she wandered through the myriad shops, specialty sections, and endless aisles of merchandise. She had the wild urge to do her next year's Christmas shopping for every member of her family. Everywhere she looked she saw the perfect gift for someone.

"Remember there'll be other places to shop," Aunt Mil reminded her. "This is only our first day."

"I *know!*" wailed Jess. "But everything's so gorgeous. It's hard to keep from splurging."

There were a few things she simply could not resist. One was a tiny Eton jacket and English schoolboy's cap for her small nephew, Chris, her sister Elsbeth's three-year-old; a set of four ecru napkins with a lace angel motif on each corner for her mother; and a cloisonné thimble for Grandmother Jeanie's collection. The silver key chain she bought for her father was a tiny reproduction of a Saxon sundial inscribed, "Peace to the Possessor," in Latin.

As she passed the tempting confectionery section, Jess gave in and sampled the delicious chocolate truffles. "To keep up my strength," she explained facetiously when Emily mentioned the possible calorie content.

But Jess defended herself, "Shopping is strenuous!"

Before leaving Harrods she made one more purchase. This time it was for herself — a beautiful pure silk scarf, bright yellow sprinkled with a pattern of butterflies.

On the street, Jess was entranced by everything — the dignified policemen known the world over as "bobbies," the red double-decker buses lurching top-heavily through the bustling traffic. The faces in the milling crowds were a grand mixture of turbaned Indians, Arabs in flowing robes, bowler-hatted bankers, uniformed schoolboys, and, of course, purple-haired "punkers."

Famished from shopping, her group was directed to a pub just off Fleet Street, the fabled "Ye Olde Cheshire Cheese" which Charles Dickens was supposed to have patronized. There, in the best British tradition, they enjoyed a typical hearty midday meal of pork pie and carrots.

"What in the world is the 'Old Lady of Threadneedle Street'?" demanded Yvonne, sliding her half-moon glasses down on her nose and regarding the others over the brochure she was holding. "This here says, 'When in London be sure to view it' — whatever that means!"

"It's the Bank of England," Aunt Mil said promptly.

"Well, for heaven's sake!" was Yvonne's response.

Since St. Paul's Cathedral and the Old Bailey were both scheduled for guided tours for the next day, the ladies lingered over coffee to discuss the question of what to do that afternoon.

"I don't know about the rest of you, but I'm worn out!" confessed Mrs. Coopley with a sigh. Emily stifled a yawn and timidly agreed she was tired, too. Even Aunt Mil admitted that she could use a nap.

"Well, I think I shall at least make a start at the British Museum. Every time I've been in London I've scheduled at least a full day there," Patricia Hollings declared superiorly.

"I never dreamed there was so much to see in a place that's smaller than Texas!" Yvonne exclaimed. "What are you going to do, Jess?"

"Well, it might sound crazy, but I'd like to shop some more," Jess said almost meekly.

"Why, honey, I'm with you!" Yvonne said enthusiastically. "I've got a pocketful of travelers checks I haven't even made a dent in yet."

So, Jess, who did not feel in the least tired, and Yvonne Trench, who declared shopping was second nature and her favorite hobby, put the other ladies in a cab to go back to the hotel. Then the two women eagerly took a bus to find fabulous fashion bargains.

The Laura Ashley Reject Shop, a postage-stamp-size store, specialized in Victorian clothes, imperceptibly flawed and sent down from their larger, fancier stores. Yvonne found adorable dresses with leg-of-mutton sleeves and ruffles galore for her twin teenage granddaughters there. Jess picked up an exquisite blouse, with tucks and hand-crocheted lace that would be perfect to wear with the velveteen "theater suit" Pam had helped her choose at Danby's back home.

At an inconspicuous little hole-in-the-wall store called "Second Act," they discovered a secondhand treasure trove. The clerk confided that most of the clothes for sale were barely worn, some perhaps only once. They were brought in by ladies of the nobility who did not want to be seen twice in the same dress. Many upper-class women regularly brought in their last-season clothes on consignment, she told Jess. "Theater people, as well." Lowering her voice significantly, she added, "Sometimes ladies of *very high rank, indeed.*"

"You don't suppose she means Princess Di, do you?" Jess giggled to Yvonne quietly as they started browsing among the racks and racks of elegant women's wear.

"Who else?" Yvonne rolled her eyes.

After a while each went off on her own to look for different things. Jess was examining a satin, marabou-trimmed evening cape, when she heard Yvonne give an excited squeal. A minute later Yvonne hurried toward her, holding out an evening gown glittering with amber sequins.

"You have to try this on, Jess!" Yvonne insisted. "It's way too small for me but it's gorgeous and a steal at the price. I'm sure it's a designer original. It looks like the kind of dress one of the movie stars of the fifties might have worn. Here." She thrust it at Jess.

Jess squeezed herself into a closet-like

dressing room and slipped into the intricately constructed gown. It had two separate pieces. The first was a crystal-pleated sheath of champagne-color chiffon lined with amber satin. Over this went a square-shouldered jacket covered with amber beads. It *was* gorgeous and, Jess knew, exactly what was being shown in the slick fashion magazines.

Staring at herself transformed, Jess's "dream-machine" clicked on. She had not a clue when or where she would ever have a chance to wear this dress, but she knew she had to buy it. The chance would probably come. After all, life had been so full of pleasant surprises recently.

Chapter Three

Two mornings later Jess woke up to the steady drizzle of rain. Her first thought was that she would have a chance to wear her new raincoat for their tour out to the white cliffs of Dover.

Downstairs in the dining room, a hearty English breakfast was set out on the massive sideboard — lamb chops, sausage and bacon, broiled mushrooms, mounds of fluffy scrambled eggs, thick slices of toast, and several kinds of preserves and marmalade. Viewing it with some awe, Jess thought it was a far cry from the juice and shredded wheat she usually had at home. As she was helping herself, Graham Campbell ambled up alongside.

"Typical tourist weather," he growled. "I should have known better than to come to England in April. It never fails. Rain, rain, rain."

"My, my, aren't we in a pleasant mood!" Jess remarked sweetly.

He looked at her startled, then mumbled, "Sorry. I guess I need a cup of coffee. English tea just doesn't do it for this early in the morning."

"I thought it was delightful," she shrugged. "I think bringing a pot of tea to each guest's room is a lovely custom. Haven't you ever heard of the adage 'when in Rome'?" Jess moved on and took a buttered raisin bun from a covered server, saying over her shoulder, "And I suppose it never rains in California?"

To her surprise Graham burst out laughing. "As a matter of fact, it does. A lot. Especially in the northern part where I live."

Jess flashed him a beatific smile and turned to take a place by the cheerful, lively Yvonne Trench at the big round table. She made a mental note to keep her distance from Graham Campbell. She was not about to let his negative comments spoil her day.

But avoiding him was more easily said than done.

Right before the time to board the bus, Aunt Mil found she had left her glasses on the bureau in their bedroom, so Jess went flying upstairs to get them for her. By the time she got on the bus Emily was sitting beside Aunt Mil, and the only vacant seat left was beside Graham Campbell.

Dismay clutched Jess grimly as she anticipated having to listen to a day-long diatribe on the tour's failings. But there was no alternative. Every other seat in the bus was occupied. After handing Aunt Mil her glasses case, Jess resignedly went back down the aisle to the empty seat beside Graham.

Graham stood up immediately and with a gallant gesture indicated she should take the window seat.

Hesitating only a split second, Jess murmured, "Thank you," slipped past him, and settled herself. Then she stared steadily out the window, into the dismal gray morning.

There was a long moment of stiff silence before Graham cleared his throat and said, "Looks like it may clear up."

Jess felt her mouth twitch at this obvious determination to be more positive. Afraid she might giggle, she made no comment.

"First off, I want to apologize!" He stopped, and a grin tugged at his mouth. "It seems that's all I do lately — apologize. I've never apologized so much to a young lady before in my life!"

Again Jess began to say something but he interrupted. "I know, I know! It certainly is required. I don't know why I always seem to come up with some kind of negative remark especially when I'd like nothing more than to agree with you!"

"It's really not necessary at all, Mr. Campbell. You're entitled to your opinion just as I'm entitled to mine," Jess replied with as much dignity as she could muster.

His eyebrow went up alarmingly. "*Mr.* Campbell? Please. *Graham.*"

Jess said nothing.

"Look here, Miss Baird. I seem to put my foot in it every time I open my mouth around you, and I'm truly sorry for that. Now, is there any other reason you find me unacceptable? I'd like it very much if we could be friends."

Jess had to admit there was something disarming about his openness. But he was so exasperating —

"Is it that you're of the Macdonald clan and I'm a Campbell, and we're not supposed to be anything but enemies? Did they brainwash you as a baby not to have anything to do with the likes of me? Never to let the memory of Glencoe die?"

"Of course not! How silly!" Jess exclaimed.

"Even though it all happened hundreds of years ago, your aunt acts as though it were a recent event," Graham said ruefully.

"You don't know Aunt Mil. She didn't expect you to take her so seriously. She has all these assorted facts on the tip of her tongue, and they just come out! And history? That's her special forte. She was a teacher for years. English and history. Naturally she's particularly interested in Scottish history. Our family, like many Scots who emigrated, are more Scottish than those who stayed in Scotland."

Graham nodded. "I know. I've had a dose of Scottish ancestry, too." He made a grimace. "Of course, according to your aunt, it's from the wrong clan."

"Oh, well, as you said, that's all past," Jess soothed. In spite of herself, she felt a smile tugging at her mouth. Maybe she had been wrong about him. Maybe there was another side to Graham Campbell after all.

"So, will you accept my apology, and can we be friends?" he persisted.

She waited as if seriously considering his request. Then she said, "Very well, yes to both questions, Mr. Campbell, if you will try to restrain yourself from a very strong inclination to make negative comments —" she said primly.

"I will. I solemnly promise," he said with mock seriousness. "Then, we can shake hands?"

"Of course," Jess laughed and held out her

hand. He immediately clasped it in a surprisingly strong grip.

Just then Peter got on the bus and Jess turned toward him, smiling. His eyes were moving over the occupants of the bus, counting heads, she imagined. Then his eyes landed on her and that sensational smile of his lit his face. Jess's heart throbbed in response.

He gave her a little nod and then said to the group, "All set for a smashing day?" With a little salute and "See you later!" he left to board the other minibus.

Regretfully, Jess thought that if Graham had not been occupying it, Peter just might have taken the seat beside her.

Surprisingly, although the converted mansion where they had been staying was in a quiet square of other stately houses, it was only a few blocks from the center of the city, and soon they were in the heart of London.

Their driver announced into his hand mike, "We'll be passing Buckingham Palace very soon, ladies and gentlemen. As you can see the house flag is flying, which means the Queen is in residence."

Jess leaned forward eagerly, peering out the window for a chance glimpse of royalty. Maybe some member of the royal family coming out through the gates on some royal errand in the Daimler?

At nineteen, the same age as Lady Di when her engagement to Prince Charles was announced, Jess had relished every scrap of newsprint about the royal romance and fairy-tale wedding. Now, at twenty-three, she could not help wondering if that kind of idyll was only to be found among royalty or in romance novels. *Love like that must be as rare as a double rainbow,* she sighed, leaning back in her seat as the bus left the city and merged onto the expressway.

Jess wondered if she would ever experience such love. She had never been able to play the game her girlfriends seemed to find so easy and natural in their relationships with boys in high school.

As a junior she had won an oratory contest with her speech based on Polonius's famous statement from *Hamlet:* "This above all, to thine own self be true,/and it must follow as the night the day,/Thou canst not then be false to any man." Jess had taken that as her guideline, but she discovered when she got to college it was even harder to apply to the dating game on campus.

"You're so transparent, Jemmy," her roommate, using her family nickname, had told her. "You really do wear your heart on your sleeve and every single emotion on your face." They had been discussing Jess's current interest in a varsity quarterback, and Donna was trying to give her advice. "You should act more cool," she had said firmly.

"But I can't be anything I'm not!" Jess had replied in despair. "I'm not cool. I'm just me."

The infatuation for the football player had only lasted the season and a few dates, and Jess, not he, was the one who had lost interest. But the fact remained that Jess had never been able to masquerade her feelings. She wanted to be accepted and liked, eventually loved, for who she was, not who she pretended to be.

"Well, lotsa luck!" her roommate had told her with a shake of her head.

Since then there had been a number of unimportant romances, most of them lasting only until Jess had frankly told the young man all she wanted was to be friends. Or until he had given up in frustration because it was clear Jess was not remotely inclined to a more intimate relationship.

Remembering all those past encounters, interludes, shortlived "fancies," Jess realized she had never really been in love.

Why not? she suddenly wondered. Not all the fellows had been hopeless. In fact, most of them had been nice looking, intelligent, personable. Yet none had created that spark, that inner knowledge that perhaps this was the special one, the person God meant for her. She had once heard Billy Graham speak to young people about their future mates. He had said something like, "Don't settle for less than God's best for you."

Maybe Donna was right, Jess thought. Maybe it would take "lotsa luck," but she preferred to believe that in God's time the right man would come into her life. She just had to be sure she was the right kind of person for him and wise enough to recognize him when he did come.

Jess sighed. It would be nice if it happened soon though. Then she remembered what her grandmother often told her: "God is always on time — never too early or too late." She would just have to be patient.

"What's that heavy sigh about?" Graham's voice interjected itself into her thoughts.

Automatically Jess stiffened. "Oh, nothing. Anyway, nothing you'd be interested in."

"How can you be so sure?" he said teasingly, but his steady blue eyes were serious.

To Jess's relief there was no time then for more conversation, for they were coming into Canterbury. They were just in time to join with another group for a "lectured" tour of the great cathedral.

The guide satiated them with a wealth of historical facts and details about the architectural features of this cathedral in contrast to other famous ones of England. In fact he was so knowledgeable and gave so many facts that Jess began to feel as if her head had suddenly become a sieve through which they were all sifting.

Finally she tuned out and simply enjoyed the awesome beauty of the arched columns, the vaulted ceiling, the spectacular windows, and the intricate carvings. She fell a little behind the others to absorb the ancient reality of the place by herself. People had actually worshiped here centuries ago. Thomas à Becket had died for his faith here.

Jess herself had never been in such a church. Her hometown church where she had worshiped all her life was simple and unadorned. Even the large church she attended after she moved to the city was plain — almost austere. As the filtered light touched the ancient stones with a mellow richness, Jess thought of the hours, days, years that had been spent creating all this beauty solely for the glory of God. The efforts of builders, artisans, craftsmen, who may have spent a whole lifetime working on this one project, seemed to merge into one splendid, tangible "Hallelujah."

The drone of the guide's voice echoed back, and it seemed almost an intrusion in the quiet, peaceful atmosphere.

When they emerged from the dim interior of the cathedral, a pale sun was trying to break through the hovering gray clouds. Surrounded once more by the bustle and conversation, Jess was jolted back into the twentieth century. The groups reassembled and got back on the bus to go to lunch at what Peter pronounced a "typically English country inn."

Gathered about one of two round tables inside the charming dining room, Jess was rather subdued. So it was with nice surprise that she noticed Peter had subtly tilted the chair next to hers to save it for himself while he settled the other group and made sure all were happily placing orders with the waiter.

Aunt Mil, the Trenches, Dr. Stavros, and Emily Mason were also at their table, and as they took their places Aunt Mil offered one of her inimitable quotations.

"As Samuel Johnson would say, 'There is nothing which had been contrived by man by which so much happiness is produced as a good tavern or inn.'"

"Hear, hear!" applauded Dr. Stavros.

"If they only served some good Texas chili, I'd be completely happy!" remarked Don, winking broadly.

Yvonne groaned and opened her menu. "He'd eat chili for breakfast if I'd serve it," she said.

Peter took his place by Jess and, as he sat down, said teasingly, "Hope you don't mind rubbing elbows with your tour guide."

Putting on her version of a Cockney accent, she replied. "Nowt 'tall. I'm that honored. You bein' a lord and all and me what's a 'umble commoner."

"I say, you're quite an actress!" beamed Peter, admiringly. "Are you keen on dramatics, that sort of thing? I mean, you're certainly pretty enough, and I must say you seem to have talent!" He laughed.

"Oh, I've done a little — bit parts in school plays. My first starring role was as Tiny Tim in Dickens's *A Christmas Carol*, believe it or not," Jess told him. "Then in the second grade I played a daffodil — or was it a banana? I can't remember. The rest of my career was usually behind the scenes. Painting scenery, moving props."

"What a coincidence. I had a few good parts myself at boarding school. Played Shylock in *The Merchant of Venice*, and later on I tried out for a really juicy part, Jack the

Ripper. But I didn't get it. Not villainous enough, I suppose."

All during the meal they carried on this kind of lighthearted banter. They chatted with the ease of two people who had known each other a long time, not just met.

When the ladies went to freshen up before boarding the bus to ride to the Dover cliffs, Aunt Mil pulled a comic face and with a pretense of severity whispered to Jess, "I'm not sure I approve of your monopolizing our tour guide, Jessamyn."

Jess laughed, knowing Aunt Mil was really delighted that she had found such a congenial companion in Peter, someone more her own age than the rest of the group.

That afternoon they all hiked along the chalk cliffs. Behind them loomed the old Dover Castle. Before them it was thrilling to see the ocean stretching far to the horizon in gray-blue stripes and the wind-driven waves crashing dramatically against the majestic rocks.

"It seems strange to think France is just over there," Jess remarked to Peter who had remained with her all afternoon.

"Yes, but I believe every Englishman, especially looking at that choppy, treacherous sea, remembers Dunkirk and the gallantry of the Dover Patrol braving it in small boats to rescue our soldiers," Peter remarked with unusual solemnity. "Uncle was one of the youngest heroes of that brave effort."

They were silent for a few minutes as if in tribute. Then Peter casually took Jess's elbow and said, "Come along. You're going to get chilled to the bone in this wind." They turned and walked back to the minibus together.

There Peter had to consult with one of the bus drivers and left Jess at the door. When she boarded she was startled to see that Graham, who had kept his distance from her since they had arrived in Exeter, was in an animated conversation with Yvonne Trench.

Jess wondered what in the world those two would have in common. But they seemed to be thoroughly enjoying each other's company.

Expecting to find Aunt Mil had saved a seat for her, Jess saw, instead, that Patricia Hollings was seated with her, and they too were chatting nonstop.

Aunt Mil was the uncontested belle of the tour, Jess suddenly realized. Everyone liked her tremendously, fascinated by her wit and her ability to come up with the oddest bits of information on nearly every subject.

With another glance around the bus, Jess observed that Dr. Stavros was holding Emily

Mason spellbound with some intensely narrated story. The Greek doctor was associating himself more and more with the Americans on the tour, mainly, Jess suspected, because of his interest in the vivacious widow.

Romance, it seemed, was about to bloom. Jess smiled to herself as she took the only empty seat left behind the driver's. And her friend Pam had predicted it would be Jess who found romance on the trip!

Well, it could happen, Jess thought with a small retroactive thrill, remembering how Peter had sought her out! Then quickly Jess scoffed. *Graham Campbell is probably right. I am a dreamer!*

Chapter
Four

Stratford-upon-Avon — Jess repeated the lyrical name softly to herself as the bus made its way through the picturesque, lush green valley of the Avon River to the town of Shakespearean fame.

The group had reservations for two plays during their stay there, a matinee performance of *The Taming of the Shrew* and one of *Hamlet* in the evening.

As they entered the town, the great modern red-brick Royal Shakespeare Theatre seemed in stark contrast to the Tudor-style houses that lined the narrow streets. This quaint little village had carefully preserved its Elizabethan streets and houses.

After a short time to settle in at the hotel, they made their way the short distance to the theater for the matinee curtain time.

The members of the Royal Shakespeare Company presented a rollicking, boisterous, hilarious show. The lead actor portrayed Petruchio with consummate skill, and a lovely actress played the rebellious Katherine as a shrew worthy of Petruchio's efforts.

Jess was a little uncomfortable with the sixteenth-century attitude toward women even in a play written at the time. But she could not help being amused and laughing when it was staged so skillfully.

It was a relaxed, happy group who gathered around the large table at the charming English tea shop later.

The interior with its Elizabethan atmosphere just suited their mood, and the tea served was exactly like that of all the English novels Jess had read. Pink and white Castle china teapots were filled with strong, fragrant tea kept piping hot by quilted chintz cozies. Baskets of scones wrapped in snowy linen were set out, along with country butter, thin-sliced homemade bread, and a variety of bittersweet marmalades and jams. Bowls of glistening, indescribably sweet ruby-red strawberries and pitchers of the famous Devon cream to pour over them topped off the elegant high tea.

The conversation was brisk, with many varying opinions on the play and its message, particularly in the light of modern perspectives.

"I doubt if any young lady in this day and age would put up with Petruchio's high-handed manner," commented Emily firmly.

"But he was so dashing! A kind of Errol Flynn type! Who could resist him?" was the surprising response of Aunt Mil.

Jess looked at her aghast. "I can't believe you said that, Aunt Mil! He was a totally insufferable 'macho' male," she exclaimed indignantly.

"But that's the way southern Mediterranean men are!" declared Patricia Hollings with the assured air of knowing she sometimes assumed.

"And Greeks, too, I'm afraid!" said Dr. Stavros with his rich laugh. "But, I'm willing to change!" he added, giving Emily a soulful look that brought color into her cheeks. A knowing glance was exchanged around the table. Everyone had noticed the growing attachment between these two.

But Jess was quickly distracted from her sentimental thoughts about them by the next comment, this time from Graham Campbell.

"I don't know whether it's so much a matter of nationality," he said with a shrug. "I suspect most women secretly like being dominated."

Jess nearly choked on her tea.

"I disagree completely!" she exclaimed more forcefully than she intended.

"Oh?" Graham turned to her with one eyebrow lifted.

"Certainly. Any woman in her right mind would object strenuously to being treated like — like an object! a slave!"

"But he was just bringing her to her senses. After all she was nothing better than a spoiled brat," Graham went on with infuriating calm.

"A man like that would be arrested for wife abuse today!" Jess declared emphatically. "No real man would want a woman who put up with that kind of abusive behavior! Certainly no gentleman would consider it!"

"No *English* gentleman, for sure," put in Peter with a chuckle.

"Oh, for goodness sake, this discussion is getting way overheated. Let's change the subject!" suggested Aunt Mil who nonetheless was enjoying the exchange.

"Yes, it is pretty ridiculous," agreed Jess, giving Graham a withering look.

"How about the play we're taking in tonight?" asked Don Trench.

"It's *Hamlet,* an Elizabethan 'whodunit,' honey," explained Yvonne, rolling her eyes as if to explain Don's lack of information.

"Undoubtedly Shakespeare's greatest play," said Patricia.

"A real masterpiece," agreed Aunt Mil.

But of course there was one dissenter. *And of course*, Jess thought, *it* would *be Graham Campbell!*

"The 'melancholy Dane'? Can you imagine a college boy coming home and claiming to see ghosts? It really stretches the imagination. I think even Shakespeare tests his staunchest fans with this one."

Jess bit her tongue. She did not want to get into another verbal battle with him, however violently she disagreed.

"Oh, but it is very believable, Mr. Campbell." This time Aunt Mil came to the defense of the play, one of Jess's favorites. "I taught high school seniors English literature, and this was a play they not only liked but could identify with! Young people have deep feelings about their parents, and they could empathize with Hamlet's distress over his mother's marriage so soon after his father's death."

For a moment Graham looked thoughtful. Then he had the good grace to concede, "Perhaps you're right, Miss Macdonald."

Aunt Mil beamed.

Jess tried to concentrate on finishing her delicious strawberries, without looking at either one. It annoyed her that Aunt Mil not only seemed to respect Graham, but actually was beginning to like the man. *Talk about a 'melancholy Dane' indeed,* she thought irritatedly. *I'd take that over a 'dour Scotsman' any day!*

On the way back to the hotel Jess asked her aunt, "Why on earth are you being so friendly with Graham Campbell? I thought you couldn't stand the man."

Aunt Mil looked surprised. Giving her niece a sharp look she said, "I think he's a very intelligent person. I like a good discussion. It gets my adrenalin flowing."

"I think he's an opinionated, hard-headed male chauvinist," retorted Jess with a little toss of her head.

"The fact that someone differs with you doesn't necessarily cut off the possibility of friendship. Personally, I find that sort of exchange stimulating."

"Peter Fortnay is much more pleasant to be with. He's never moody or impatient. He's always charming —"

"But that's his job, dear!" protested Aunt Mil mildly.

Jess started to say something, then stopped. Could Peter's seeking her out, being so attentive and charming be just a part of his job as tour guide? Surely not! He must find her interesting and attractive to choose to spend so much time with her.

Not wanting to explore the possibility that he didn't, Jess thrust her annoyance back and went to bathe and dress in happy anticipation of the night's theater experience.

As the members of the tour were finding their places at the theater that evening, Peter put his Playbill program on the seat beside Jess before going to see that all the others in the group were comfortably seated. Jess looked up a few minutes later to see Graham standing before the vacant seat.

"I'm sorry. But Peter will be along in a minute."

Graham's jaw tightened noticeably. "Oh, our amiable tour guide. He seems to have become your constant escort," he remarked edgily.

Jess felt a surge of indignation. What business was it of his if Peter chose to view the play beside her?

"Well, enjoy yourselves," Graham said. Then he turned and walked back to the end of the row, sat down, and buried his head in the program.

What a short fuse the man has! Jess thought in annoyance. It was such an effort for him to be gracious. But she was just as irritated that Graham almost always managed to disturb her in some way.

To everyone's surprise the theater manager announced that due to the sudden illness of two of the actors in major roles the evening's scheduled performance of *Hamlet* would be canceled. Instead, they hoped the audience would be pleased by the substitution of the universal favorite *Romeo and Juliet*.

After an initial ripple of disappointment the audience settled down and soon became enthralled. Jess was immediately caught up in the play, totally absorbed as the familiar story of the two families of Verona and their ancient feud came alive with the magic of the fine actors and the deathless beauty of the lines.

Jess found herself completely captured by the haunting, bittersweet poignancy of the final act. As the house lights went up she discreetly wiped tears from the corners of her eyes. She was unable to immediately detach herself from the illusion of the play back to reality. Although she was familiar with the story, tonight's performance had deeply moved her. She had been touched as never before by the drama of the star-crossed young lovers.

Peter murmured, "Excuse me, I must go see about the —"

The rest of what he said was lost. Jess, trying to recover her emotional balance, reached for her jacket and gathered up her small velvet clutch bag and program as Peter departed.

"Beautiful, wasn't it?" asked a familiar voice, and Jess looked up to see Graham standing at the end of the row of seats as if waiting for her.

As she moved toward him he put his hand gently under her elbow. Without another word, he guided her down the aisle and through the milling crowd out of the theater.

The night was clear, and a damp, refreshing wind was blowing as they walked silently toward the hotel. Jess appreciated Graham's quiet acceptance that she did not feel like talking. Maybe Aunt Mil was right. She was a good judge of character. Perhaps there was a sensitive, intuitive side of Graham Campbell.

The other members of the tour were clustered in the lobby of the hotel, outside the lounge.

"We're all going in for a nightcap," Don Trench greeted them jovially.

Jess hesitated. She wasn't sure she wanted to be with everyone. Somehow she wanted to keep the lingering beauty of the play intact. She had the feeling Graham was reluctant, too, but with everyone looking at them expectantly, they couldn't refuse.

Even this lively crowd seems somewhat subdued tonight, Jess thought, as she looked around the table and sipped her espresso. Only Aunt Mil and Graham seemed inclined to get involved in conversation.

"I walked around a little this afternoon and everywhere I looked I saw the title 'The Bard.' I know they mean Shakespeare, here, naturally, but for a good Scotsman the real 'Bard' is Robert Burns. Right, Miss Macdonald?" he asked.

Aunt Mil nodded her head vigorously.

"Spoken like a good Scotsman. Of course," she said to the others, "he wrote the most beautiful love poems."

"Could anything be more beautiful than Romeo's comparing Juliet to a rose?" asked Dr. Stavros of the romantic, dark eyes.

I think Burns's 'my luve is like a red, red rose' is equally beautiful," Graham said, and for some reason Jess felt an instinctive response.

"And of course, every Scot anywhere celebrates the Bard's birthday on January 25th!" declared Aunt Mil. "When I was growing up, it was almost as big a celebration as Thanksgiving or Christmas in my family."

"Mine, too!" laughed Graham. "Even in California, Scots gather to have a big birthday party in his honor."

"You certainly remember that, too, Jessamyn?" Aunt Mil prompted.

"Sure, Aunt Mil." She remembered it vividly. All the men in the family dressed in full Highland regalia — kilts, tartans, and sporrans. The women wore their finest formals, usually in the colors of the clan's tartan. The children were always encouraged to come and be part of the celebration.

Aunt Mil began to delight the group with tales of the traditional "hurling of the haggis," and she soon had everyone laughing. Suddenly, in the middle of the merriment, Jess instinctively looked over at Graham who was enjoying the story as much as the rest. *What a wonderful smile he has,* she thought. *It totally transforms his face!* Graham was actually very handsome, she realized with some surprise.

At that moment he caught her glance, and for the second time an indefinable but intrinsically powerful current passed between them. It was so strong, Jess drew in her breath and had to look away. It came and went so quickly she could not grasp its meaning. She would try to figure it out later.

Soon afterward, the party began to break up, each person saying sleepy goodnights and exchanging comments about the tour plans for the next day. They would be going to the nearby Warwickshire village of Shottery just a mile west of Stratford-upon-Avon. There they would see the thatched-roof cottage that Anne Hathaway had lived in until she married William Shakespeare.

Although Jess had promised herself to think about the strangely intimate glance she and Graham had exchanged and what it could possibly mean, she fell asleep before she could form a thought. It probably was her imagination anyway, she decided drowsily.

The next morning Jess woke early, got up, and dressed. Aunt Mil was still sleeping when Jess tiptoed out of the room and went down to the hotel dining room to have a cup of coffee.

Sitting at a corner table looking over the playbills from the night before, Jess had no idea of what a charming picture she made when Graham, standing at the entrance, saw her.

Morning sun slanting in through the window touched her dark hair with shining highlights. The soft cowl collar of her cinnamon cashmere sweater framed her small face becomingly.

He had never noticed how long and curved the lashes of her wide blue-green eyes were until she looked up at him, startled, when he walked over to her table and spoke.

"Good morning, Miss Baird," he said cheerfully.

"Why, good morning!" Graham was smiling broadly, and again Jess thought what a difference it made in his looks.

"May I join you for coffee, or would you rather be alone?"

"No, please do," she said, feeling suddenly shy. He was looking at her so — so *how? Tenderly?* No, that couldn't be it. She felt herself blush, but thankfully Graham had turned to signal a waiter and didn't see it.

"I've been wanting a chance to—" he began, pulling out a chair opposite her. But Graham never sat down, for at that very moment the Trenches and Peter walked into the dining room.

Yvonne waved and smiled and called to them. "Good morning! Let's find a bigger table so we can all have breakfast together!" she suggested.

Jess heard Graham suppress a groan, a low "Oh, no!"

But Yvonne was already instructing the waiter to bring a big pot of coffee and beckoning to Jess. The only polite thing they could do was get up and move over to the large table in the center of the room.

Before long the other members of the tour had joined them, and a short time later they were all boarding the minibuses for Shottery.

Yvonne had hold of Jess's arm as she had not finished a long, involved story about her shopping trip for souvenirs for her grandchildren. So when they got on the bus, they naturally sat together.

Graham, looking glum, stalked past.

When they got to Shottery, Aunt Mil and Emily came up to Jess and Yvonne and they all walked together to Anne Hathaway's cottage. Graham was trailing behind with Don and Dr. Stavros. Peter was herding the Baults and the others.

But when they got to Anne Hathaway's home, Emily had the brilliant idea of posing Jess and Peter at the gate while she snapped a picture. It was a little embarrassing for Jess, but she complied.

"It will be so — so *significant* to have two young people standing before the home where Shakespeare courted Anne Hathaway," said Emily as she angled her camera at the two.

Peter took it in his stride. And when Emily chirped, "Get a little closer, please," he obligingly put his arm around Jess, giving her a hug.

"Oh, that's *darling!*" squealed Emily happily. "Now, just hold still for another snap, just in the case this doesn't come out!"

At this point, Graham growled audibly. "Theirs wasn't exactly a love match, you know." With that he plunged his hands in his jacket pockets and marched off.

Jess looked after him, irritated.

He kept his distance most of the afternoon, only showing up again when they were standing reading the epitaphs at Shakespeare's gravesite.

"It's amazing how many famous men had wives named Anne," Aunt Mil remarked. "Anne Hathaway, of course. Anne Boleyn, Anne Morrow Lindbergh, to mention a few." Turning to see Graham, Aunt Mil commented, "You were right, Graham. It wasn't exactly a love match. Imagine his leaving her his *second*-best bed in his will!"

"It seems she got his second best in everything," Graham agreed. "She certainly wasn't the mysterious Dark Lady of his sonnets."

Her curiosity piqued, Jess asked him directly, "How do you know so much about this?"

His face reddened a bit. "I teach English literature at a small college."

A professor! Jess almost gasped. *He doesn't look old enough,* she thought. Then she remembered that first day when she had asked him if he was a writer and he had said something about making a critical survey — of course. It had somehow slipped her mind.

Just then Peter came up, "Enjoying yourself?" he asked Jess.

Happily Jess smiled. "Yes, thoroughly. Everything's great!"

"Good, I'm glad," Peter said, and he tucked her hand through his arm. They started walking down the cobblestone street toward the minibus. "You're going to love our next event. A real medieval banquet in an authentic castle!"

Basking in Peter's flattering attention Jess never saw the mixture of emotions on Graham's face as he watched them. But Aunt Mil did.

Chapter
Five

At Jess's first sight of the ancient castle with its climbing turrets, mullioned windows, and battlemented tower, she felt she had stepped into the pages of her favorite childhood fairy tale.

They arrived in the late afternoon, and the sun glinting on the paned windows made them sparkle like diamonds. It also gave a roseate gleam to the lovely gray stone.

Set like a precious jewel on dense green velvet, surrounded by magnificent old oaks, the castle rose, silhouetted in majestic splendor against the pastel sky.

Two liveried footmen came running down the terrace steps to take charge of the luggage as the group emerged from the two minibuses in a kind of hushed awe.

Jess hardly dared look at Aunt Mil as they were ushered up shallow carpeted steps balustraded by lacy stonework, down a long hall, around two turns, through a carved walnut door, and into a high-ceilinged, spacious bedroom. A huge bed, canopied in embroidered damask, a massive armoire, a mirrored dressing table, and a marble fireplace with a glowing fire greeted their stunned gaze.

The footman who had carried up their bags opened a door to a beautifully appointed bathroom and then, bowing slightly, said, "I hope everything is in order. If there is anything you wish, please ring." He indicated a tapestry bell pull by the fireplace. "Tea will be sent up directly," he added as he noiselessly left the room.

As soon as the door closed behind him Jess spun around and threw out her arms and demanded excitedly, "Aunt Mil! Have you ever seen anything so fabulous?"

Even Aunt Mil seemed impressed by the grandeur. "I never imagined it would be anything like this, to tell you the truth, Jessamyn. And to think we are here due to my facility for remembering bits and pieces of trivial information!"

"Remember, you always told us, Auntie, 'Nothing you learn is ever wasted'? So, you've proved your point!" laughed Jess.

A few minutes later a discreet knock sounded at the door, and a maid, dressed in gray uniform, with an organdy apron and fluted cap like a paper muffin cup, entered with a tea tray. After a murmured greeting, she placed it on the low table in front of the fireplace, then quietly withdrew.

Seated opposite her aunt on one of the damask chairs on either side of the fireplace, Jess watched her pour steaming tea from a graceful silver pot into shell-like porcelain cups as though she had been doing it every day of her life.

"This is unreal, isn't it?" Jess demanded wonderingly, glancing about the elegant room. "I don't know why I'm whispering!" she giggled. "Maybe it's because I keep thinking suddenly I'm going to wake up and find this was all a dream!"

Aunt Mil smiled at her indulgently. "It's real enough, Jessamyn," she said, handing her a teacup.

There were dainty little sandwiches and small diamond-shaped cakes, with pastel icing and tiny candy flowers on top.

"Did I thank you enough for bringing me along, Aunt Mil?" Jess sighed happily.

This time her aunt chuckled. "You did, Jessamyn, several times."

"I don't know how I can ever thank you enough, though," Jess remarked as she took another watercress sandwich.

"Just by enjoying yourself every minute," Aunt Mil told her. "That will be all the thanks I want or need."

After tea, Aunt Mil wanted to bathe and nap before dinner.

Jess went over to the blue moiré silk-covered chaise lounge and stretched out. Raising her arms above her head she looked around the room and smiled, comparing it to her small apartment with its thrift-shop furnishings and calico curtains from mill outlet stores. It was bright and colorful and filled with things she loved, but after this — ?

Jess sighed and asked herself. *How on earth will I ever go back to my Cinderella life after all this?*

It was a kind of rhetorical question. But on the other hand it needed an answer. Jess had left a lot of unfinished business behind her. There were questions she would have to face when she got back — like what to do with the rest of her life?

For some a straight course seemed to be charted. Jess had watched some of her friends finish school, get a job in a chosen field, eventually marry, and start a family. That's what her sister Elsbeth had done. And she seemed sublimely happy doing it.

Elsbeth never seemed to have any problem dealing with life. But then she didn't have Jess's restless, romantic nature.

It really sounded simple enough. But for Jess it wasn't. Her biggest puzzle had always been what she should do with her life. She had been brought up to believe that God has a plan for everyone. All you have to do is find it, focus on it, and then forge ahead. The trouble was that so far Jess had not been able to do that. That was the reason she had dropped out of college after two years. She didn't really know what kind of career she wanted to pursue or what courses she needed to lead her into something meaningful. So she had decided to get a full-time job and try her wings living away from home.

The sudden layoff was now forcing her to make new plans. Maybe she would go back to college and get a degree. But in what? The experience of working, being on her own, and handling her own finances had matured her, made her more responsible. But as for her future, Jess still was unsure.

With half-pensive amusement Jess was reminded of the droll quote on a coffee mug someone had given her for a joke, "Now that you've got it together, where you goin' to put it?"

That was exactly the question Jess knew she would have to answer after the tour.

Just then Aunt Mil peered around the

76

edge of the door and said, "Better start getting ready, Jessamyn. It's nearly seven, dear."

So Jess rose, mentally putting thoughts about an uncertain future on the back burner. That could wait. Tonight was just to enjoy.

Jess was glad she had thrown caution to the wind that day in London when she had bought the beaded amber dress. She had had second thoughts every time she had taken it out of her suitcase and hung it up in the various places they had stayed on the tour. But now she had no regrets. The impulsive purchase was the perfect choice for tonight's festive affair. She had never had such a dress and probably never would again, so she was going to wear it and enjoy it.

But even Jess was amazed at what it did to — or rather for — her appearance. The wisp of sophisticated glamour completely changed her look.

"Why, Jessamyn, you look so . . . so grown up!" exclaimed Aunt Mil as Jess turned from the mirror. "You're very lovely!"

"Why thank you, Aunt Mil, But it's mostly the dress," she told her aunt. "A dress like this would do wonders for anyone."

But Aunt Mil, although she said nothing, knew otherwise.

There was a new sparkle in Jessamyn's eyes. The new glow of her complexion was more than the English climate — which was supposed to be so good for the skin — could offer. There was something else new about Jessamyn lately, and Aunt Mil wasn't quite sure what it was.

She did know that the slender, shining young woman was at the peak of blooming beauty and vibrance, and all the more charming because she wasn't even aware of it. Nor was Jess aware of how two young men were both understandably attracted to her.

If Jess had had the slightest doubt about her appearance or the success of her dress, it would have been immediately whisked away by the appreciative look Peter gave her when he saw her coming down the stairway and hurried over to meet her.

He took her hand and in his assured British accent echoed her aunt's compliment, "I must say, Miss Baird, you look incredibly beautiful this evening."

A kind of blissful warmth rushed through Jess, bringing a lovely color into her cheeks.

Peter himself looked splendid in a black dinner jacket, white ruffled shirt, and black bow tie.

"Shall we go in?" he asked.

Taking his arm Jess felt like a real princess being escorted by as handsome a prince as she ever imagined in any long-ago fairy story.

In fact it was the perfect beginning to an evening that might have been a tale spun by a master storyteller. In a castle where King Henry IV might have visited, a magical background of music played on ancient instruments transported the participants into a gone but not forgotten era of chivalry and romance.

The dining hall was tremendous, with a high vaulted ceiling and tall arched windows. Flaming torches in wall sconces cast a flickering, shadowed light.

From their place in a mounted recess, a group of musicians in velvet doublets and shoes with turned-up toes were playing a soft, lovely medieval ballad on antique stringed instruments.

Along with Jess and Peter, the other members of the tour, all formally dressed and a little subdued by the pageantry into which they had suddenly been conveyed, took places at the T-shaped table covered with a crimson, gilt-embroidered cloth. They had just relaxed in high-backed, velvet-upholstered chairs, each one like a throne, when a master of ceremonies stepped in front of the little band of musicians. He declared in a loud voice, "Now, let the festivities begin!"

At once serving maids in colorful laced bodices, ruffled blouses, and full skirts began bringing in huge platters of roasted meats, vegetables, and fruit. Large trays loaded with uncut crusty bread and the local cheese were set down near bowls of butter churned in the castle dairy. Before each guest, the maids placed a tankard of mead, the medieval drink of fermented honey.

Jess, always willing to try something new, took one sip and immediately decided the people of the Middle Ages were made of sterner stuff. Peter laughed at the face she made as she pushed the pewter mug away.

The genial master of ceremonies, who was playing "host" of the castle banquet, instructed them that to really get in the mood of things, they should try serving themselves and eating in the authentic style of the olden days — with their fingers! This suggestion was greeted with much laughter and loud protests from the assembled company.

"For those more modern souls," their host placatingly added, "our pretty serving wenches will pass among you with damp scented towels on which to wipe your dainty fingers!" This sly insinuation that they might not be good sports produced further merriment.

"It's hard to overcome a lifetime of ingrained table manners," Peter admitted to Jess as he gingerly picked up a chop dripping with gravy and leaned forward over his plate. Since she was attempting to manage a similar trick and not soil the amber gown, all she could do was nod encouragingly. Amid much laughter, other members of the party were having the same difficulties.

"Didn't he say we could sop up the juices with bread?" asked the soft-voiced Mrs. Coopley plaintively.

"Nothing to it!" hooted Don Trench. "It's just like a Texas barbecue back home."

"I thought this was the time when knighthood was in flower and all those lovely damsels were in distress," wailed Emily, struggling with some dripping meat.

"I can see why they were in distress! No napkins," joked Aunt Mil.

"All that's missing is a pack of hounds stalking around the table waiting for the scraps and bones," said Patricia Hollings with the superior air she used when she wanted to impress them with her knowledge, this time of the strange customs of life in medieval castles.

"Ugh!" groaned Yvonne, fastidiously waving her fingers after a try at eating. "I think I'd trade all this quaintness for a paper towel." Then she added with her usual good-natured grin, "But this is a lot of fun!"

After they all had eaten as much as they could manage or dared to, the table was cleared and their host stepped up on the raised platform with the musicians and announced, "And now the dancing will begin. These dances will be new to you, but easy enough to learn. In medieval times dancing, most of which was imported to England from France, was an art that every lady and gentleman acquired. It was also an honored way of making your romantic attentions known to the lady of your choice. So if you will all choose partners, we can begin the instruction."

All the married couples on the tour got up, some rather reluctantly. But urged on by their mates, they joined in the spirit of the festive evening. Dr. Stavros, with his continental bow, claimed Emily, and they took their place on the polished parqueted floor.

"I'm sorry, but I should really see that all the unattached ladies don't get left out. If any are without partners, it's really my duty to dance with them," Peter whispered apologetically to Jess. "Besides, I don't think you'll be lacking a partner."

Jess turned to see what he was looking at over her shoulder, and to her surprise she saw Graham's tall figure approaching. But before he reached her side, Patricia Hollings stood up, blocking his approach.

At the same time, Peter spoke again. "Well, it looks like everyone's taken care of after all. Let's go and see if we can execute a medieval dance."

Peter shifted her chair and put out his hand to Jess, assisting her to rise. He slipped his arm around her to lead her out onto the dance floor.

It was then Jess saw Graham halt midway toward her. In another second she saw Patricia Hollings stepping out as the dance partner of the master of ceremonies himself.

The look that flashed across Graham's face was a mixture of disappointment, chagrin, and anger. He turned and walked back to his place at the far end of the table.

What is he so angry about? Jess wondered. Was it something Patricia had said, or had Graham been coming to ask her to be his partner? Jess was puzzled and unsure, but did not have any time to figure it out, for Peter was whisking her off to join the other couples.

Learning the intricate, measured steps of the medieval dances took all her concentration, and thoroughly enjoying the challenge, Jess did not have a chance to think any more about the enigmatic Graham Campbell. In fact, she looked around for him once or twice later, but he was nowhere to be seen.

What is the matter with the fellow? Jess asked herself, half irritated that it should bother her. Why couldn't he just relax and enjoy himself like the rest of them? In any case she was sure that whatever had upset him had nothing to do with her.

Jess was soon distracted from her random thoughts about Graham Campbell by Peter's compellingly flattering attention. She was swept up in the frivolity of the evening. Looking into Peter's smiling eyes as they danced, she felt she had never been so happy.

The dances they were taught had a flirtatious element. With Peter as her partner Jess felt an excitement — a provocative pleasure. His hand was gentle on her waist as they made the turns and bows. Then at the finale he swung her up in his arms, swirling her around, then setting her down in a kind of embrace. Jess's heart was pounding. She felt breathless, dizzy.

When the master of ceremonies announced the next dance would be the last one of the evening, Peter took Jess's hand

and led her out on the dance floor. This dance had the dancers form an arch with their hands under which the partners went joining the line at its end. Peter's eyes never left Jess's face as they held hands on opposite sides of the arch. When it was time to promenade, his arm around her waist was firm.

"I hate to see the evening end. I've had an absolutely smashing time. I don't know when I've enjoyed anything so much."

When the music came to a stop, he lifted her hand to his lips and kissed the fingertips. It was enough to go to any damsel's head, Jess thought deliriously.

Finally the gala evening was over. As everyone straggled wearily off to bed, they all declared it had been the highlight of the tour so far.

Later on, back in her bedroom, Jess sank into one of the comfortable chairs, kicked off her satin sandals, wiggled her toes luxuriously in the thick Oriental rug, and sighed ecstatically. "What a glorious evening, Aunt Mil! Everyone had a marvelous time! That is — except—"

"You mean Graham Campbell?" her aunt asked sharply.

"Of course. Who else? He wouldn't even

try learning the dances! Did you notice? Just tramped off, and disappeared for the rest of the evening."

"But he was green with jealousy, can't you see that? I'm amazed you didn't realize he's been attracted to you from the very first day. I recognized his approach. Oh, he's a 'canny Scot,' all right. All those little remarks to get your sparks flying, to see if you're a lassie with spirit. Can't you see how he never lets you get far out of his sight if he can help it? He was probably planning to take his own sweet time, but Peter Fortnay's interest in you has him worried. He hadn't counted on that kind of competition, I'm sure."

Jess looked at her aunt in amazement. "Why, Aunt Mil, I can't believe it! I'm sure Graham Campbell only thinks of me as a star-struck romantic young girl! Sure, he likes to needle me, see my reactions to his remarks. I grant you that! But after all he's a college professor, writes books, I think. At least he's gathering material for some kind of critical survey —What in the world would he see in someone like me?"

"Believe it, Jessamyn. His kind of man is awkward when it comes to women. He's actually like a little boy for all his degrees, expertise, and high IQ. I know the type. I didn't teach school for forty years for nothing," Aunt Mil said with authority. "Graham Campbell is more than just a little interested in you, my dear."

Tired as she was physically, Jess still felt too wide-awake to go right to sleep. Long after Aunt Mil was soundly sleeping, Jess got up quietly, went over to the casement window, and leaned on the stone embrasure to look out into the lovely spring night.

The words of the homesick poet Robert Browning writing from Italy — "Oh, to be in England, Now that April's there" — floated through Jess's mind. How lucky she was and how grateful to Aunt Mil for making it possible.

And thank you, Lord! she whispered softly, with a heart full of wonder and gratitude for all her blessings.

As she lingered at the window her attention was drawn to a figure on the terrace below, a tall, angular, familiar figure. Slowly she recognized Graham Campbell!

So Graham had not gone to bed early, after all. For there he was fully clothed, wide-awake, and as unable to sleep as Jess herself had been. Why?

Holding her breath she watched him pace the length of the terrace with long strides, then turn and walk back. His hands were clasped behind him. His head was bent as if he were in deep thought. Then he halted and stood looking at the sliver of moon shining through the lace foliage of the ancient oaks.

Jess drew back into the shadow of the alcoved window in case Graham should look up suddenly and see her.

She felt the stirring within her of something so slight and fragile that she was only marginally aware of it. Could it be possible, *just possible*, that she and Graham were kindred spirits? Two romantics sharing the delight of a pale new moon in a lilac sky?

Chapter
Six

The first thing Jess heard as she woke the next morning was the sound of steady rain. It made the day's plan to tour the castle from tower to dungeons even more spectacularly spooky.

Since the castle had its own staff and tour guide, it seemed quite natural when Peter fell in step alongside Jess as part of the rest of the group.

The history of the castle was fascinating. Originally it had been a Cistercian abbey for monks. Its complex of buildings made up almost an independent village in itself. The monks had tended farmlands, pastures, and gardens in addition to maintaining church, gatehouse, chapter house, separate kitchen, and bakery. Much of the abbey had been destroyed during the sixteenth-century reign of Henry VIII. He ordered the dissolution of the monasteries and confiscated church properties. The place was then sold to one of his court favorites. That nobleman built this large castle from some of the stones of the ruined abbey.

As they followed their guide down winding, barely lit, treacherously steep stone stairways to the dungeons, Jess clung dizzily to the rope banister. She was grateful for Peter's steadying hand under her arm. Although it was magnificent, there was something eerie about the place, she decided. The day outside was gray, and pale light coming through the high, narrow windows made the castle seem even gloomier. The magic of the night before seemed to have disappeared in the cold light of day. Perhaps its history gave the place the haunting atmosphere.

Probably because of Aunt Mil's surprising statements concerning Graham, Jess was more aware than ever of his presence. But he made no effort to approach her. In fact, he seemed to be purposely keeping his distance. Whenever she looked his way, he seemed to be examining one of the messages carved in the stone walls or reading one of the several descriptions of dungeon life. Mentally Jess shrugged, more sure than ever that Aunt Mil's imagination was working overtime. Not only was Graham not interested; but he was also obviously indifferent.

No, there was no figuring out the fellow, Jess decided with a sigh. It was so much easier to be with the charming, uncomplicated Peter. She certainly did not need a brooding Scot in her life.

After the chilling experience of viewing the dungeons where the former lords of the manor had incarcerated their enemies and sometimes forgotten them for years, the paneled library upstairs was a welcome change. A crackling fire was burning in the huge stone fireplace.

After a delightful tea of bread, cheese, and preserves, Peter announced a tour of the abbey ruins and grounds within the hour. Those hearty souls who wanted to brave the harsh, drizzly weather were welcome.

"Are you game?" Peter asked Jess. "Or have you had enough of the gore and lore of this ancient place?"

"Well, I don't like to miss anything!" she said.

Peter smiled. "Good for you! What a sport you are, Jessamyn."

That was the first time he had called her by her first name, and Jess's heart gave an excited little thump. Peter seemed to realize it, too, and said quickly, "*May* I call you Jessamyn?" Spoken in his lilting English accent, her name had never sounded so pretty.

"Yes, of course," she replied, feeling herself flush.

"Excuse me for a few moments. I must make a telephone call. Shall we meet in the great hall in about half an hour then?" suggested Peter.

When Peter left, Jess helped herself to another crumpet and was standing near the fireplace sipping her tea when Graham ambled over to her.

"Well, what do you think of the plain truth of how the English nobility acquired their land and property? Has it damaged any of your romantic notions yet?"

Jess bristled. Why did this annoying man always assume something about her without any evidence? Did he think she was a fool who couldn't separate history from fiction? Before she could think of an adequate counter for his remark, Aunt Mil joined them.

"My word! But those dungeons made me shudder," she said with a little shake of her head. "It certainly brings stories like *The Man in the Iron Mask* and *The Three Musketeers* to life."

"*The Three Musketeers!*" repeated Graham. "I loved that story when I was a kid! My brother and a buddy of his and I used to play that all the time. But I can't think of the names of any of them except D'Artagnan —"

"D'Artagnan, Porthos, and Aramis," Aunt Mil supplied promptly.

Graham looked shocked. "That's remarkable!" he said, gazing at her in admiration. "I'd never have thought of them. I'd have had to look it up!"

Aunt Mil looked smugly pleased.

Jess looked at Graham with new interest. "You must have been quite an imaginative little boy. What else did you play?" she asked, half-teasingly.

"My brother was the one who usually thought up the games. He was two years older and the leader. Let's see, Robinson Crusoe, of course—"

"Who was actually a fellow Scot, you know," interjected Aunt Mil. "He was William Selkirk, a Scottish sailor, who spent four years alone on an island off the coast of Chile."

This time Graham looked stunned. "I don't believe this!" he exclaimed.

Aunt Mil just chuckled.

Graham put his head on one side and with a cautious eye said slowly, "We also used to play *Treasure Island* in the summer at the beach. You wouldn't happen to know the name of the ship they sailed with Long John Silver and—"

"Captain Smollett of the *Hispanola*," Aunt Mil finished for him.

"I am truly speechless!" Graham declared. "What a phenomenal memory you must have."

"Well you see I taught school for a good many years and am fairly familiar with English literature which was the main reason I chose this particular tour—" began Aunt Mil.

"But Aunt Mil is a storehouse of other facts," interrupted Jess. "You can't stump her."

"I wouldn't want to try," Graham said solemnly.

All three of them laughed.

For the first time since she had met him, Jess felt a bond of camaraderie flowing between Graham and herself. He was smiling at her with genuine warmth and seemed just about to say something more when Peter came up with Jess's coat over his arm.

He nodded affably to Graham, then turned to Jess. "All set? The rest of those who are going on the abbey tour are waiting in the hall." He turned to Aunt Mil. "Are you going with Jessamyn and me, Miss Macdonald?"

Aunt Mil never blinked an eyelash, and only Jess noticed the smallest twitch of her mouth as she replied, "I believe I'll skip this one, Captain Fortnay. I have some postcards to write and I may take a short nap."

"Right, then. Coming, Jessamyn?" He held out her coat for her to slip into as he asked Graham, almost as an afterthought, "And you, Mr. Campbell, are you taking this one in?"

Graham suddenly seemed remote. "I'm not overly fond of touring desecrated churches. I take a dim view of Henry VIII's way of paying off political debts. I think he would have done better to reform the clergy more and places of worship less." He spoke with a grim intensity. Then as if aware of the effect his speech had had on a startled Peter, he added more calmly, "I may look around on my own later." With that he turned on his heel and strode off.

Peter lifted an eyebrow to Jess and winked at Graham's departing back. "Wow, I'd say that fellow has definite opinions." Then he smiled and took her arm. "Come along, Jess. For all that, they are worth seeing —"

Although Jess went with Peter she felt a kind of nagging discomfort as she remembered Graham's words. Clearly he was a man of strong convictions, unswerving

95

principle. She found that admirable. It was just that — what? She was uncertain exactly how she did feel about Graham Campbell.

The tour of the ruined chapter house, refectory, and chapel was interesting, but even in Peter's enjoyable company, Jess came away feeling vaguely depressed. Ironically, she found her thoughts returning constantly to Graham Campbell. What an enigma he was.

This afternoon in his conversation with Aunt Mil he was interesting and delightful. Then that inexplicable change came over him when Peter had joined them. He was certainly a man of many moods. Difficult! Well, there was no point wasting time trying to figure out someone who had accidentally stumbled into her life. After the tour was over, she would never see him again.

But as Jess dismissed Graham from her mind, the thought of Peter took its place. After the tour would he also disappear from her life?

It was a dismaying possibility. Of course, she knew she and Peter came from two different worlds. His was the privileged one of English aristocracy — of nannies and nursery teas, of being educated at a prestigious "public," which actually means private, school before entering university, and of a carefully structured social life. She knew none of these things.

Still she knew instinctively that Peter found her attractive, interesting, and fun to be with. He had told her that in so many words, and his eyes told her more. But the tour was half over, she knew, and what then?

It was something she didn't want to think about. At least, not yet. Not now.

Even though Jess did not want to think about it then, the next day she was forced to when she overheard a conversation between Yvonne Trench and Patricia Hollings.

Jess had boarded the bus early and taken a seat in the back. Today they were taking a day-long trip to the legendary Sherwood Forest, and Peter had already informed her he would be riding on the other bus. The Baults and Dr. Stavros were not familiar with the escapades of the famous band of English outlaws and their leader Robin Hood, and Peter felt he ought to be with them to explain.

"Besides, I have to spend my time fairly, you understand. My personal preference would be otherwise," he told Jess with a regretful smile.

Yvonne and Patricia boarded the bus

busily chatting, completely unaware that anyone else was there.

At first, Jess wasn't paying any attention to their chatter. Then she suddenly realized she and Peter were the subject of it. As she did her ears perked up and her face flamed.

With a sickening sensation, she knew she was on the proverbial horns of a dilemma. If she made her presence known, everyone would be horribly embarrassed. If not, she could not escape listening. She slid farther down in her seat, wishing desperately that she could be invisible.

Totally unconscious of their listener, the women, seated up front, continued talking.

"He's what I call a lady-killer," Yvonne said decisively.

"I've seen this sort of thing a dozen times," Patricia Hollings said knowingly. "It's very common. A young, impressionable girl, and an experienced charmer."

"Well, he's sure loaded with charm, all right," Yvonne declared. "In Texas we'd say he could charm the bugs right off a potato vine." She laughed, "If I were a few years younger and single I might fall for him myself."

"If she were more sophisticated, worldly, and realized this kind of romance only lasts the length of the tour, then . . ." Patricia's voice trailed off regretfully.

"Maybe her aunt will talk some sense into her. Or maybe she's well aware of what she's letting herself in for. Who knows?"

The bus soon began to fill up with other passengers, and no one noticed that Jess had already been there. As usual the conversation was lively, with jokes, comments, and cheerful exchanges. All were anticipating the day ahead.

Thankfully, no one seemed aware of Jess's unusual quiet. Inwardly she was seething, furious to be the topic of gossip. Realistically, she knew that in any small group everything was observed, and perhaps it was only natural that the two youngest members on the tour had gravitated toward each other.

But it isn't a romance, for goodness sake! she thought indignantly. And she wasn't head over heels in love with Peter Fortnay as Yvonne and Patricia assumed. At least, she didn't think she was!

Of course she was flattered at his interest. But what woman wouldn't enjoy a charming, handsome young man's attention. That didn't mean she expected anything to come of it! That would be crazy! An impossible dream!

She tried to shake her annoyance at being gossiped about by Yvonne, whom she genuinely liked. And as for Patricia Hollings, who cared what she thought, Jess shrugged.

By the time they had reached the beautiful Sherwood Forest, the setting for one of Jess's favorite childhood stories, she had regained her natural good humor and was able to reply pleasantly to Yvonne's friendly greeting.

"I thought you were probably on the other bus with Peter," she said with some surprise.

Jess passed off the query casually and went to join Aunt Mil and Emily as they started down a lovely trail, to the Council Oak, wishing something would happen to someone else and divert attention from her.

Something did. And it wasn't something Jess would have wished. Aunt Mil, turning to make some remark to Emily and Dr. Stavros who were behind her, tripped on a tree root, stumbled, and fell, twisting her ankle painfully.

Luckily the Greek doctor was in immediate attendance. He whipped out his large, linen handkerchief and wrapped her rapidly swelling ankle tightly. Then with Jess on one side and him on the other, they assisted her back to the bus.

With her foot elevated on the seat across the aisle, Aunt Mil insisted she would be fine. She wanted them to finish the hike. After Dr. Stavros was assured that as soon as they returned to the castle she would apply ice packs and allow him to bandage it properly, they did as she requested.

That evening as they gathered before dinner in the great hall, as the castle's drawing room was called, Aunt Mil was treated like a queen. Sitting in a tapestried chair, she was showered with solicitous inquiries and brought hot tea. Dr. Stavros and Graham helped her into the dining room.

Jess made a mental note of telling Aunt Mil she was entirely wrong about Graham Campbell's having any interest in *her*. As a matter of fact, he had ignored her most of the day and now was devoting himself exclusively to Aunt Mil.

Of course, with Peter seated beside her at the dinner table, Jess had plenty of attention. But it piqued her a little that Graham had not so much as given her a glance. It also annoyed her that great peals of laughter came from his end of the table. And she could not hear or share the conversation at the other end.

Jess certainly meant to ask Aunt Mil what all the hilarity was about later. But she didn't have the chance. After dinner, when the others were all having their coffee together in the front of the roaring fire, Peter drew Jess into the hallway.

"You know the next week is going to be spent at Fortnay Hall, our family home," he began. "I talked to my uncle this afternoon, and he's feeling marvelously fit again, back problems all gone. But he's going to need some help getting everything organized when the tour arrives. So I'm going on ahead there tomorrow to see about things."

"You won't be going with us to the Brontës, then?" Jess asked, disappointed.

Their schedule called for them to drive north the next day to Haworth in the Yorkshire dales, a tour stop which Jess had been eagerly anticipating.

"No, but there are guides, there, you know. And you're all getting to be experienced travelers, so being on your own won't be any trouble." He paused. "You'll just follow the tour schedule. Then you'll come on to the Hall." Peter took both of Jess's hands. "Oh, Jessamyn, I can't wait for you to see it. I know you're going to love it. You're so responsive, so appreciative. I'm going to adore showing you around. This is one part of the tour I am an expert on!" He smiled down at her, his dark eyes warm, eager.

Jess felt a rush of excited anticipation. There seemed something significant in

Peter's eagerness to have her come to Fortnay Hall, his ancestral home. "Oh, Peter, I know I'll love it!"

They stood there smiling at each other, and for a long moment, Jess had a strange sensation that she was spinning happily in space.

"You're really quite marvelous, Jessamyn," Peter said softly, and in a dazzle of delight Jess was sure he was about to kiss her.

Then a voice from behind them shattered her golden bubble of happiness. "They're looking for a fourth for bridge in here. Is either of you interested in taking a hand?"

Jess stiffened and turned slowly to see Graham Campbell standing in the doorway of the library with a glint in his eyes that she could not quite discern. She gladly could have strangled him!

Chapter
Seven

"I really hate leaving you, Aunt Mil; most of all, I hate the fact that you're missing this special part of the tour!" Jess said sadly as she got ready to leave for Haworth.

"It can't be helped, dear. Dr. Stavros says I must stay off my foot until the swelling goes down entirely. I can't disobey doctor's orders, can I?" she chuckled. "Anyway, you can tell me all about it when you get back. In the meantime, I'll be reading this!" She held up a copy of *Wuthering Heights* by Emily Brontë.

"Guess who was thoughtful enough to get it for me?" she asked slyly, her blue eyes twinkling merrily behind her glasses.

"I haven't the faintest idea. Dr. Stavros?"

"No, Graham Campbell," Aunt Mil replied, watching for Jess's reaction.

"Oh — him!" shrugged Jess.

"Yes, I thought it was awfully kind."

"Unexpected, too," Jess retorted as she snapped her suitcase closed.

"I like the man . . . more and more," Aunt Mil said firmly.

"Well, I'll leave you to your book and your own opinion," Jess said teasingly. She bent down to kiss her aunt's cheek before she went out the door, down the steps, and out to where the two minibuses waited.

Perhaps of all the places on the tour Jess had looked forward most eagerly to visiting the Brontë parsonage, the home of the tragic sisters, all writers, and their feckless brother Bramwell. Jess had read most of their gothic novels and a recent biography of the most famous one, Charlotte.

When Jess had got on the bus, everyone else was already settled, and she took the only seat left behind the driver. She noticed Graham was sitting with Emily and across the aisle from Patricia Hollings, and they were all vigorously discussing the Brontë sisters and their writings.

With the drone of the bus motor loud in her ears, Jess could only hear a dull murmur of conversation behind her. She felt sorry Aunt Mil wasn't along, and she missed Peter more than she had expected she would.

Jess looked out the bus window as they got farther into bleak Yorkshire country. At the sight of the rolling moors, she felt a shiver of expectation, and as they entered the somber cobbled town with its grey stone houses, Jess was experiencing a sense of pilgrimage.

As the group started up the walk to the drab, brooding house, where the Brontës once lived, Jess felt a sort of awe that was rudely violated when she overheard Graham. "They were all terribly neurotic, you know," he was saying. "All that morbid brooding, anguished passion, and unrequited love they wrote about was surely the result of warped, emotionally unbalanced minds—"

Unable to stop herself, Jess whirled around and demanded, "Why must you spoil everything for everyone else? I can handle being disappointed in something *after* I've seen it. But to have something ruined for me beforehand is unbearable! Must you always air your jaundiced opinions about everything?"

Graham looked stunned at first, then stricken, then remorseful.

This time Jess did not wait for his apology. Leaving a shocked silence behind her she almost ran to the door of the house.

Jess kept a careful distance from both Graham and the others while they went through the home of the doomed Brontë family. Here three young women had lived out their tragic lives and written their haunting novels and poems. She did not want anything to distract her as she tried to imagine what each room must have been like for these creative souls, isolated as they were and feeding on fantasy to produce stories that lived long after themselves. She lingered in the museum next door to the shabby house to look over the exhibits of some of the original manuscripts, photographs, and other prized possessions of the three talented sisters who had died so young.

When the guide suggested some of them might want to walk up on the moors to the site of the old farmhouse, the real Wuthering Heights, Jess was enthusiastic to do it. But the weather had turned ugly. Rather than brave a cold, dank, misty fog, most of the tour members decided to go to a nearby tavern for warm drinks instead. The guide told them the tavern had been frequented by Bramwell, the Brontës' flawed genius of a brother.

"It's been turned into a fine restaurant and inn now," he assured them. "You'll find it a cheerful place to wait by a nice fire while the hardier ones tramp over the moors."

Among the handful who decided to brave

the climb up the hill was, to Jess's dismay, Graham Campbell. She started ahead, walking fast, but his long legs soon brought him alongside her, and he quickly matched his steps to hers.

"Miss Baird —" he began, but she stared straight ahead and increased her pace. "Jessamyn — Jess! Please listen to me. I'm sorry about what happened a while ago. I never meant to spoil anything for you! Honestly! Please believe me."

She walked even faster, but he caught her arm and halted her, saying, "I want you to know how I feel."

Forced by the strength of his grip to stop, she faced him angrily. They were far enough away from the Coopleys and Dr. Stavros and Emily so that no one could hear her as she spoke in a low, level tone.

"Really, Mr. Campbell, I am not interested in your excuses or in how you feel. I just want to be able to enjoy this tour in my own way. So let's just leave it like that. Do you think you could manage to do that?"

"I understand how you feel—" Graham started to say, but Jess cut him off.

"How in the world can you say that?" she demanded. "You don't know how I feel! You couldn't and say the sorts of things you do about places and people I admire!"

She started walking away from him again as rapidly as she could. He was right on her heels. He put out a restraining hand and caught her arm. Annoyed, she stopped and turned. "What is it?" she frowned.

"At least give me credit for being genuinely repentant!" Graham said humbly. "Would you believe it may be because I'm a 'closet' romantic myself and overcompensate by making remarks like that. Actually, it's probably a cover for my own tendency to relate to these emotional Victorians." His smile was sheepish.

She pressed her lips together tightly, not wanting to relent, but he persisted. "Please, it's really important to me that you do understand."

"Why on earth is it important that I understand?"

"Because . . ." he hesitated, "because I'd like very much for you . . . to like me. To know I'm not all bad. That I have some redeeming qualities — even if they haven't been very evident up to now. From now on, I promise not to make any more negative remarks."

Jess had to laugh. "Given your past performances, I don't think that's a promise you can keep."

"Well, let's say I'll try — very hard!" He

109

was smiling now, and again Jess noticed how good-looking he was when he did. Little crinkles formed around his laughter-filled eyes, and straight, white teeth flashed in his grin.

"Okay," she said slowly.

"It's a deal?"

"A deal," she agreed, laughing.

"I'm a man of my word!" persisted Graham.

"All right!" sighed Jess, and she began walking.

"You know, I am an instructor and we're inclined to take attitudes, play devil's advocate sometimes, to get our students to think things through and not just accept a writer or playwright on the basis of current acceptance or acclaim! Maybe I've carried it too far — on this tour, at least. Probably I should try to look at things with a fresh eye, with no preconceived theories."

Again Jess stopped and regarded him in perplexity. "Oh, for goodness sake, must you make everything so complicated?" she pleaded. "Isn't it enough just to enjoy some things for their own sake?"

He looked back at her steadily, then said, "Of course. You're absolutely right."

They started climbing the hill which was

becoming rocky and thickly grown with wild, tough grass.

At the top Jess stood looking about with a sense of wonder. Here, at last, were the moors of which she had read so much and so often. Their remoteness was awe-inspiring. She could almost see the slender figure of Emily Brontë roaming up here with her dog, as lonely a spirit as the loneliness of her surroundings. Intense, imaginative, restless, peopling her books with memorable characters born out of these very hills, she evoked emotions that countless readers would find echoed their own yearnings for love.

Just then Dr. Stavros shouted from behind them, "We're going back. Emily's cold!"

"I'm freezing!" called Emily, waving as she turned around. It looked like the Coopleys were going back, too.

The sky was an ominous shade of gunmetal gray, with heavy dark clouds scudding in. It was windy and cold, but Jess had no intention of giving up now that she had come this far.

On the top of the craggy hill, the wind was a cutting knife, penetrating even Jess's thick sweater and raincoat. It rose in a high, keening wail like the voices of all the lost and tragic souls Emily Brontë had written about. In spite of herself, Jess shuddered, and a second later she felt Graham's arm go around her shoulders. He pulled her against him, sheltering her from the sharp edge of the wind.

Startled, she leaned against him, momentarily warmed by his tall, solid body shielding her from the piercing chill.

Surprised at her own reaction to this unexpected closeness, the sense of kinship in being here together, alone, in this forsaken place, Jess held herself motionless. Then she pushed back and stepped away from him, and Graham reluctantly released her.

The wind was making an awful tangle of her hair, and Jess pulled out her yellow silk scarf to try to tie it around her head and keep it back. But the strength of the wind whipped the fragile silk from her hands and sent it sailing into the air like a bright, yellow kite. Graham made a flying grab for it, but the wind carried it off. The last they saw of it, it was sailing over the moors.

Jess stood for a minute looking after the disappearing scrap of silk, then shrugged.

"That's too bad," Graham commented sympathetically.

"Well, after all, it was only a scarf and not very expensive at that," she laughed. "Anyway, I've left a piece of myself on an English moor."

They smiled at each other there on that windy hill. For a split second Jess felt the same stunning impact as that first day she had looked out the bus window in London and met Graham's eyes.

"Come on," he said finally, breaking the tingling moment. "It's really raw up here. We'd better start back or you'll never get warm."

As they started down the rocky path together, it seemed quite natural when he put his arm around Jess's waist, holding her firmly as they maneuvered the stones and rough moor grass.

It started to rain harder. With icy drops pelting their faces, they ran until, laughing and breathless, they reached the end of the path. Then they stopped short.

The street near the parsonage was empty. Both minibuses were gone.

"They must be parked near that tavern," Graham suggested. "Let's go see."

Jess turned to look back at the Brontë house but by now it was darkened and deserted. Tourists and guides had all disappeared.

"Come on, or you'll get soaked." Graham grabbed her hand, and they began to run again down the cobblestone street toward the lighted windows of the tavern.

Chapter
Eight

The weathered wooden sign over the tavern entrance was swinging wildly in the wind as Graham pushed open the door and they both rushed inside in a gust of rain.

"For pity's sake!" exclaimed a stout, red-cheeked woman behind the reception desk. "You two look nearly drowned, for sure!"

"It is a bit wet out there!" Graham laughed agreeably, rubbing his hands together.

"Well, come along in then. I'll get you somethin' to take the chill out of your bones," she said coming out from behind and starting into the pub section. "What'll you be drinkin'?" she asked.

Graham turned to Jess questioningly.

"Something hot — nonalcoholic," she said.

"Make that two. Coffee or tea," he said to the woman.

"How about mulled cider?" she asked.

"That sounds great. Right, Jess?"

The woman eyed Jess severely.

"You, Miss, would you like to freshen up, dry your hair, maybe?"

Jess put her hands up to feel the wet mass of tangled curls.

"That might be a good idea."

"The 'ladies' is just around the corner there, dearie."

Jess started in that direction, then turned to Graham.

"Hadn't we better ask about the buses?"

"What buses are those, dearie?" the woman asked.

"Our tour buses," Graham replied. "We think they may have gone off and left us."

"Stranded, are you?" she clicked her tongue sympathetically. "Were they on the tour to the parsonage?"

"Yes."

"Well, there were several groups in and out all day. But the last bunch left quite awhile ago. Two parties of about five, one earlier and one just about half an hour later."

"They're not in the dining room then?" Graham asked.

The woman shook her head.

"Just had drinks, then were on their way. How's it happened they left the two of you?" she was curious.

"I guess both of them thought we were with the other group. That's the only way I can explain it." Graham shrugged.

"What will we do then?" asked Jess, frowning.

"Just wait here. Have a good hot supper. They'll soon discover the mistake and send someone to get us. It's only a little more than an hour and a half's drive." He smiled at her. "I never question fate. Maybe it could even be considered good luck."

"Good luck?" she echoed.

"Having a chance to get to know you better," he grinned, "and for you to get to know me."

With only an amused smile for a reply, Jess started toward the restroom.

After she had done what she could to untangle her curls, she joined Graham in the pleasant warmth of the inn's restaurant. He was sitting at a table near the crackling fire in the fireplace.

He stood and pulled out the chair beside him facing the fire. Jess looked about her appreciatively.

"Speaking of ports in a storm," she smiled, "this couldn't be a nicer place to find refuge."

"I wish I could remember your aunt's appropriate quotation from Samuel Johnson about the English inn," Graham said.

"I can't remember exactly. Something about it being — no, I can't quote it. But then Aunt Mil has so many," she laughed.

"She is a fantastic lady."

"Once you called her 'formidable,' " chided Jess.

Graham winced. "You have a formidable memory! I wish I could wipe out your first impression of me and start all over."

"My first impression was nice," Jess told him, thinking of that moment from the bus window. "It was my *second* impression you'd better work on erasing."

Just then their cheery hostess bustled up with their mugs of steaming mulled cider.

"Well, now, you're both looking a lot better. Here's your cider. What would you like to eat? We've got a choice tonight, lamb stew or shepherd's pie, both real tasty."

"Shepherd's pie? That's—" began Jess.

"Tender beef and mutton chunks baked with potatoes, peas, and carrots in a flaky pastry shell, then covered with whipped potatoes," the woman finished for her.

"Sounds delicious."

"It is."

"Very well, I'll have that, too," Graham said.

When the woman had left with their

order, Graham said teasingly, "See how agreeable I can be?"

"And now," he said, folding his arms on the table and leaning forward, "let's get down to the business of getting acquainted."

"I feel as if I'm being interviewed," Jess said, feeling suddenly shy with Graham observing her so intently.

"Not at all. Actually, I know quite a bit about you already from your aunt."

"You've been talking to Aunt Mil about *me?*" she gasped.

"Oh, very discreetly. I don't like being obvious."

Jess sipped the sweet, spicy apple drink, contemplating Graham over the rim of her mug.

"Your aunt tells me you won all sorts of debating prizes in high school, several essay contests —"

"Oh, she didn't!" Jess exclaimed in dismay. "Just wait until I see her."

"She's properly proud of you, that's all."

"But that must sound so — so juvenile to someone like you — a college professor!" declared Jess, feeling her face grow warmer.

"Please, don't be put off by that. Contrary to what you said earlier about my making everything so complicated, actually I'm a very simple guy." There was something roguish in Graham's smile.

"Simple?" echoed Jess, striking her forehead in mock despair. She was thinking she found him as complex as a character in a Henry James novel.

"Quakers believe it's a gift to be simple," he said thoughtfully. "Maybe that's something I'd like to cultivate." He paused. "Now, please tell me about yourself." He looked at Jess with interest.

"I'm not very mysterious. In fact, people have told me I'm very transparent — what you see is what you get!"

"I can see you have a quick, curious mind, an interest in everything, a fine intelligence."

"Not really. Actually, I'm not even well educated, just well-read," Jess told him. "Certainly, not compared to someone like you — a college instructor," she pointed out, eager to turn the conversation away from herself. "What do you do besides teach?"

"Run on the beach — I live in a house on a cliff overlooking the ocean," Graham said, "— browse in secondhand bookstores on rainy Saturdays, roam through junk stores searching for odd pieces of furniture I can refinish, go to foreign movies, to the planetarium to look at stars —" He broke off. "Sounds boring, huh?"

"Not at all. I was just thinking—" began Jess, but did not have a chance to finish what she had been about to say because their dinners arrived.

What she had been thinking during Graham's recital was how similar their tastes were.

Jess was hungrier that she had realized and the shepherd's pie was delicious. The afternoon on the moors had given them both a hearty appetite, and as they ate Graham said, "About education, I've found it's relative. I mean degrees only mean something on paper. What really counts is what you've actually learned. You see I went to college on an athletic scholarship, and for the first year it didn't mean all that much to me. Then, I suddenly got 'turned on.'" He stopped chuckling. "— and I was cut from the team."

"You were!" Jess was shocked. She had thought Graham was about to tell her about a football career. "Why?"

"I found I liked other facets of campus life more than practice eight hours a day. Coach said I lacked team spirit. I guess that was the first real stirring of the 'rugged individualist' I became," Graham said, laughing self-deprecatingly.

"The truth is I just didn't want to spend

all my time on the practice field. You see, I'd been excited by some of the courses I was introduced to at the university, and that seemed more important than making a field goal. I could see the coach's point."

Right then their waitress came with a small coffeepot she set on a candle burner, then asked them if they were ready for dessert. "Apple tart?" she offered.

"Too full." Jess shook her head.

Graham hesitated, then said, "No, thanks, I'll pass."

That word triggered Jess's curiosity.

"So what happened after you flunked football?" she teased.

"Are you sure I'm not boring you?" he asked.

"No, I'm interested. Really," she assured him.

"Well, when I finally made it through college — which wasn't all that easy for me, the Vietnam thing was on. I didn't like the idea of going into the army and probably being sent over there when I wasn't sure we were there for the right reasons. Anyway, I chose alternative service and ended up teaching on an Indian reservation for three years. It was the best learning experience I could have had. Wonderful people. They taught me a lot." He paused reflectively as if remembering a very special time in his life. "After that I taught in an inner-city school for two years before going back to the university to get my master's."

"It sounds as though you've been very busy. Too busy, I suppose, to get —" Jess stopped short, realizing what she was about to say.

"Too busy to get married?" Graham finished it for her. "You wonder why I'm not married?" he asked.

"Well, yes." Jess felt embarrassed now that the subject had been opened.

"The answer is simple. Cowardice." He grinned.

"You're afraid?"

"The statistics *are* pretty frightening. Especially in California. One out of every four marriages ends in divorce."

He went on, "For me marriage would be a one-time, lifetime commitment. Finding someone who feels the same isn't exactly easy nowadays."

"You must be a Christian," Jess blurted out impulsively, then could have bitten her tongue.

Graham's gaze leveled on her steadily as he answered. "I am. A recent one, but nonetheless a convinced one. I had what I guess you'd call a kind of crossroads experience a couple of years ago. You know, about what I should do with my life, how best to invest it. I was feeling burned out and went through a real period of soul searching. I needed time to put my life together in a meaningful way." He paused. "I discovered that I could only take it one step at a time. You don't rush spiritual growth."

There was a long pause. Then Graham said with a slight smile, "I'm still trying to find out what life is all about. I'm beginning to believe it takes a lifetime of learning, seeking. But there's one thing I'm very sure of, and that is the only thing worth living for is something worth dying for — a belief, a conviction. For me it is a commitment to Christ and finding the best way to serve Him as an individual." He paused again. "I guess I know that my own happiness is not an end in itself."

Jess felt a spontaneous urge to tell Graham that she too was in the process of searching for direction. Actually, praying for guidance. It surprised her that she would want to share that with him. But he had been so open, so honest about himself she felt a sudden confidence that he would understand. And the fact that he was a Christian made all the difference.

She opened her mouth to speak, but at the

same time the front door blew open with a great rainswept wind. It banged loudly against the wall as it was yanked out of the hand of the slicker-coated man who had just walked through it.

Both Jess and Graham jumped. When they turned to see what had caused the noise, they saw the driver of their minibus.

Cap in hand, wiping his rain-wet face with a big red handkerchief, he advanced toward them, his poncho dripping water on the polished oak floors. The hostess followed him in, clicking her tongue, stooping every so often to swab at the puddles of water he was leaving in a trail behind him.

"Sorry, Miss; sorry, Sir!" he apologized. "Everybody thought you wuz in the other bus from theirs. Nobody thought to check. 'Twasn't till we wuz back and your aunt, Miss, asked about you that we figured out what 'appened. Sorry as I can be. But I turned right around and drove straightaway back."

Graham assured him, "'All's well that ends well' as our friend Will would say." He gave Jess a broad wink.

"Well then, I'm ready to start back any time you are," the man said.

The arrival of the driver ended the unexpectedly intimate time they had shared together, and Jess felt somehow cheated. She would have liked to talk longer, but the mood had been abruptly broken.

Although Jess did not realize it then, she had made two startling discoveries that afternoon, one about Graham and another about herself. But there was not time to examine them yet.

The next day they were on their way to Fortnay Hall and to Peter.

Chapter
Nine

Winding in and out rolling, endless acres of velvety green parkland dotted here and there with groves of lovely old trees, the tour bus finally rounded a curve bordered with hedges of lilac, azalea, and flowering rhododendron bushes. At last Fortnay Hall came into view.

It was a gracious mansion of rosy brick, a rambling building of indeterminate architecture, looking as though it might have been added on to as need demanded, but still having a proud character of its own.

Terraced gardens descended along vine-covered gray stone walls to the river that looped at the back of the sweeping lawn.

But there was no sign of Peter. Instead a tall, silver-haired gentleman, with a distinctive military bearing, in a khaki safari suit came out of an arched, carved door. He was followed by a butler in morning coat, gray vest, and starched bat-winged shirt, and also by two uniformed maids. He came down the shallow, stone steps, leaning slightly on a cane and greeted each guest as they got out of the minibuses.

"Welcome to Fortnay Hall. Terribly sorry not to have been on hand when you first arrived! But I imagine Peter did an admirable job, didn't he? We will certainly see to it that the rest of your visit is splendid! Hope the journey wasn't too tiring. For now, we'll just see that you're shown to your rooms, given time to bathe and rest, and then we'll all gather for a social hour and to get acquainted."

Colonel Fortnay was what Peter might be in thirty years, Jess thought. Handsome, suave, correct, with just the right mixture of friendliness and dignified reserve.

As she stepped inside the dark walnut-paneled hall, Jess had the impression of magnificence. There were gold-framed mirrors, huge flower arrangements in priceless vases on museum-quality antique tables, a massive double staircase leading upwards to a gallery and a balcony that circled the hall.

Imagine! This was Peter's home growing up! Jess mused, wondering what it was like for a little boy to live here.

But then, she reasoned, probably all his

friends had houses much like this, and he thought nothing of it. Just as she had not thought the homes of her childhood playmates much different from hers in their pleasant suburb.

The tour group gathered around Colonel Fortnay while his well-trained servants began to sort and carry up luggage to the assigned rooms. Two by two the tourists followed them, slowly, lingering to point out something to each other, such as the breathtaking carved ceiling with its flowers, gilt medallions, and figures. Some paused to examine the fine paintings that hung in the upper hall.

Jess and Aunt Mil were shown to adjoining bedrooms handsomely furnished in massive Victorian mahogany. The high beds, with their ornately curved headboards, were piled with lacy pillows and fluffy satin comforters. They looked so inviting that Aunt Mil decided to have a nap before dinner.

But Jess was far too excited to think of resting. Instead she changed into a luscious periwinkle blue sweater dress that she had not yet worn on the trip and went downstairs. She wanted to look around on her own and just maybe run into Peter.

Downstairs, on either side of the entrance hall, were the drawing room and the dining room, splendid with formal furnishings and crystal chandeliers. They looked as untouched and as austere as museum displays. Surely there must be living quarters for the family apart from these, Jess thought, as she stood gazing into the dining room as if at a movie set. She walked out onto the terrace overlooking the beautiful formal gardens. She leaned on the stone balustrade and breathed in the soft spring air. Below a lone gardener worked among the flower beds.

As she watched he moved slowly, steadily, until he was weeding directly in front of her. Jess leaned over the railing and spoke to him, "These gardens are lovely. You certainly do a marvelous job keeping them."

The man squinted up at her, then stood up. He pushed back the brim of his hat with one hand while he took a large handkerchief out of his overall pocket and wiped his face.

"Mebbe," he commented. "But not like in the old days. It's too much work with too little help. We used to have eight gardeners working five days a week with me the head gardener. Now I've only got two helpers come mebbe once or twice a week." He shook his head sadly, "No, Miss, it's not like the old days. Money's scarce and help not dependable, slipshod. But money's the main problem. That's why his lordship opens the house to tourists and travelers. Might not be able to keep it anyhow if things get any worse."

Jess couldn't think of anything comforting to say. The man was obviously getting older, and these acres of shrubs and flower beds were too much for him. There was something familiar in what he said, and Jess recalled it was much the same sort of thing Graham talked about. England was in a serious recession.

As if aware he might have said too much to a stranger about the affairs of his employer's family, the gardener picked up his tools and walked away from the terrace and began to work at a distant flower bed.

"Hello there!" A voice spoke softly behind her.

Jess whirled around and almost into Peter's arms. "Oh, my, you startled me!" she gasped.

He put both his hands out and rested them lightly on her shoulders. "Sorry! And sorry I wasn't here to welcome you. Something came up and I had to leave for a while. I wanted to be here when you came!"

Jess's eyes danced happily. "I was just admiring your house — your home, I mean!"

Peter winced. "These are the public rooms, the ones people come gawking through twice a week. I'm sure Uncle means to entertain before dinner upstairs in our — I think you'd call it in America — the family room."

"I can't believe there's any room in this place that could accurately be compared to any American family room, Peter!"

Peter looked puzzled but went on, "Anyhow, these rooms are just for show. We do have living quarters that are less formidable. I do believe Uncle plans to have dinner down here tonight though." He smiled a bit apologetically and said, "It does impress the tourists."

"I don't doubt it. *I'm* impressed," Jess said solemnly. "Actually, this is the way I always thought royalty lived, to tell the truth."

"Well — perhaps, *minor* royalty," he conceded, "although, I know my great-grandfather did entertain royalty. As a matter of fact, King Edward VII was often a guest here. He liked shooting, you see, and our woods are filled with quail and deer, so he would come periodically. Don't misunderstand. The king and my great-grandfather weren't close friends. But it was considered a very great honor to have him as a guest, even though it was quite expensive to do so. All sorts of protocol had to be observed. It was the custom for the king to send down a list of those whose company he would enjoy, and then it was up to the host to invite, prepare, and plan for that number."

"In other words, royalty's friendship had its price."

"Yes, indeed. There's no telling what the expense of that kind of a visit might amount to, because all the king's friends brought their own retinue of personal servants with them. These had to be housed and fed as well," Peter explained.

"I see." Jess started to ask if Colonel Fortnay had ever entertained the present royal family but decided such a question might not be in good taste. However, Peter brought up the subject himself.

"Of course, none of that sort of entertaining is done here anymore. Not anywhere in England nowadays." He took Jess's arm and suggested, "Would you like to walk out in the garden? It's really lovely now that spring has come."

" 'Oh, to be in England, Now that April's there!' " she quoted softly.

"You always say just the right thing at the right moment, don't you, Jessamyn?" He took her hand as they walked out through the door onto the stone-flagged terrace.

"It's just that I really love your country, Peter! Browning and all your poets." She looked up at him smiling. "I'm only repeating the words they've written."

"Still you have a talent for enjoyment I find truly remarkable," Peter said admiringly.

Jess almost said, "But it's being with you I'm enjoying." Her feelings about Peter were too new, too unexplored to express. All she knew was that with him she felt lighthearted. She certainly felt none of the tension she felt with Graham Campbell!

The formal gardens were laid out with gravel paths between borders of colorful blossoms. The waning sunlight, the flowers, the vivid greenness of the precise hedges, and the stone benches set into arches lent an old-fashioned charm and aura as they walked along. Behind them the pink stone mansion seemed part of a dream.

Suddenly Peter halted, glanced at his wristwatch, and exclaimed impatiently, "Sorry, Jessamyn, I didn't realize it was getting so late. I must go change for dinner. Uncle expects me to do the honors when we all gather in the lounge."

He held her hand a minute longer. Before he let it go reluctantly, he said, "Did I tell you I missed you?"

Jess shook her head.

"Well, I did." His smile caressed her. "It

surprised me no end! But I did!"

They both laughed lightly.

"I'll see you later." Peter gave her a small salute, then turned and walked back toward the house.

What a splendid figure he cut in his riding clothes, the handsome fitted jacket, faun-colored breeches, polished boots! He looked as right in this setting as if some artist had included him in a painting titled "English Gentleman, Country Estate." Perhaps, the only thing that was missing was someone waiting in the doorway to greet him.

"PUT YOURSELF IN THIS PICTURE" was an advertising slogan Jess once saw in a travel agency window over a poster of a sunny beach. In the center of the picture was a mirror so that any passerby stopping to gaze longingly saw his own image reflected. The same image crossed her mind as she stood looking at the stately mansion into which Peter had just disappeared.

"PUT YOURSELF IN THIS PICTURE." The phrase repeated itself in Jess's thoughts. *What would it be like to live in such surroundings?* she wondered. A gentle breeze rustled the glossy leaves of the pink and purple rhododendron. Overhead a flock of English robins swooped down to the lily pond filling the soft spring twilight with their sweet, high twittering.

You dreamer! Jess taunted herself. But somehow in this environment, even the wildest dreams seemed possible.

That evening Jess felt somewhat distracted as she dressed for dinner. She wore the royal blue velveteen suit and paler blue blouse, ruffled at throat and wrists, that she had worn to the Royal Shakespeare Theatre for *Romeo and Juliet.* It made her feel feminine, romantic — exactly the way she wanted to feel here at Fortnay Hall, and she fairly floated down the stairway and into the lounge.

Peter, who seemed to have been watching for her, came right over to her, his eyes registering compliments, his smile welcoming. He drew her hand through his arm and led her over to the refreshment table, asking, "What will you have? Sherry? G and T? Tomato juice?"

He pronounced it "to-mah-to," and Jess unconsciously did the same when she replied. "Tomato juice, please."

He poured it for her and handed her the glass. "You look simply smashing," he told her. "In fact, I'd say England agrees with you remarkably well. You look even prettier than the first time I saw you, and I thought then you were one of the prettiest girls I'd ever seen."

Jess sipped her juice to cover a combination of pleasure and shyness that swept over her. Was it England or Peter's obvious interest that had given her a new radiance that even Aunt Mil had mentioned?

At a burst of laughter from the other side of the room where Aunt Mil was surrounded, Jess glanced over. Aunt Mil seemed to have a circle of admirers, among them Colonel Fortnay and Graham Campbell. Peter, noticing it too, remarked, "Your aunt has quite a charming way about her. It must run in the family," he said.

"Aunt Mil is a wonderful storyteller with a great sense of humor," Jess commented with a little twinge of curiosity. What *was* Aunt Mil regaling them all with now?

She did not have a chance to find out then for Peter made no attempt to circulate impartially as he had previously. He was leaving the hospitality to his uncle and focusing his attention solely on Jess. When dinner was announced and they all went in Peter made sure she was seated beside him, and he devoted most of his conversation to her.

Down the table Jess could hear snatches of the lively, laughter-filled banter between the colonel, Graham, and Aunt Mil. Once she heard the Colonel declare, "This lady simply cannot be stumped! I've never seen anyone like her."

"Of course not," Graham agreed. "She was the undisputed champion —"

At that point Peter had asked Jess a question. Turning to answer, she missed the rest of Graham's remark. She could not help wondering if Aunt Mil had told them about winning the trivia contest. She was such an unassuming person Jess doubted if she had. It would have seemed too much like bragging.

Another time, however, Jess did hear this bit.

"Who was President Roosevelt's famous pet?"

"A Scotty — Fala."

"Elizabeth Barrett's dog?"

"A cocker spaniel named Flush."

"How about Samuel Johnson's cat?" someone asked.

"Hedge!" said Aunt Mil triumphantly.

More laughter was sprinkled with a spatter of applause.

By this time they were through the first three courses of clear veal broth, then salmon and squab — both from the estate, Peter informed Jess. The fresh vegetables were also grown on the farm. A lovely flan with hothouse peaches was served for dessert.

"After we've finished, I know my uncle is going to suggest cards in the library. But I'd like us to slip away to the Fortnays' 'Rogue's Gallery.' I'll try to impress you with my gallant ancestors," Peter said in a conspiratorial tone.

So instead of following Colonel Fortnay with the others, Peter took Jess's hand, and they ducked down the hall, then up the winding stairway to the gallery on the second floor.

The gallery was, indeed, impressive with arched beams and the rich, dark paneling hung with huge portraits in heavy gold frames.

"Jessamyn, I present to you the Fortnays," Peter said with mock formality, giving a sweeping bow.

"You said you would try to impress me. Well, Peter I *am* impressed," Jess said with dramatic awe in keeping with his theatrical stance.

Actually she was. They walked slowly around, stopping here and there as Peter told her some of the life's story of one of the handsomely attired men or gorgeously gowned, bejeweled women. The Fortnay family had been painted in almost every generation of British history. At one more modern portrait they halted, and Peter explained this was his own grandfather. He was in a uniform, complete with gold epaulets, laden with medals, and he wore the wide blue sash of a Knight of the Garter. His wife, Peter's grandmother, was a lady of great beauty. She wore the gown she had worn for her formal presentation at court. It was a shimmering satin with a swirling train. The requisite three white plumes rose from her tiara.

"Oh, Peter how perfectly exquisite!" Jess exclaimed. "What a thrill that must be to be presented to the king and queen. Do you have to be royalty yourself or what?"

"You usually have to be sponsored by someone who is of the nobility or married to a noble," Peter replied. Then he turned to her, took both her hands in his, and said, "I should like to see you gowned like that, Jessamyn. You would look stunning. I can almost see you. . . ."

They stood gazing into each other's eyes while crazy thoughts whirled in Jess's head. *Imagine!* she thought, *My being presented to the queen! Lady Jessamyn Baird!* She almost laughed out loud at the idea.

Peter, standing very close to her, reached out and traced the line of her cheek with one finger, saying very softly, "I love your blue-green eyes. They are sparkling now like stars, and —" His finger was at her hair line now. "I love your smile and your mouth . . ." Peter was whispering, and Jess felt small, chilly tremors as he took her gently into his arms and kissed her slowly.

She did not resist, not even a little. She simply responded to what seemed perfectly natural. The kiss was thrilling and deeply sweet. When his lips moved from hers, Peter spoke. His voice was husky as he said, "I do think I'm falling in love with you, Jessamyn."

Jess's heart began to thud rapidly. She lifted her face to look into Peter's.

Suddenly they heard footsteps coming up the stone steps and Colonel Fortnay's booming voice. "I'm glad you asked to see the family portraits. I don't like to impose my ancestors on anyone unless they really want to see them. Now, here we are, sir!"

Jess moved out of Peter's arms just in time to see Colonel Fortnay reach the top of the steps with Graham Campbell just behind him.

Chapter
Ten

In the tradition of the English manor house, early morning tea was brought to the guests' rooms. On her tray Jess found a single red rose and a note from Peter.

"I'd like to give you a personal tour of Fortnay Hall today. What would you say to taking a 'holiday' from the others' schedule and coming with me? Send word back by Emma, if you will."

Jess quickly scribbled "Yes!" on the bottom of the note, folded it again, and handed it to the rosy-cheeked waiting maid. Afterward, Jess wondered if that had been the correct thing to do, not the going but the way she had replied. English people were so keen on doing things correctly. Perhaps she should have used her own note paper to answer.

Oh, for goodness sake, Jess! she scolded herself impatiently. *You are going overboard!*

*Probably what Peter likes about you is your nat-
uralness — your American-ness, if there is such
a word!*

She tried on and discarded three different
outfits before deciding on the blue cashmere
sweater set, her "find" at London's Westway
and Westway store. She added a lightweight
grey flannel skirt and her Frye boots.

Brimming with her plans for the day, she
popped her head into Aunt Mil's room. Not
waiting for the expected teasing comment,
she blew a kiss, then ran downstairs where
Peter was waiting in the lower hall.

Dressed casually in a dark blue cable
stitch sweater and buff slacks, Peter greeted
her with that special smile that did weird
things to her breathing. "Come along, I
want to show you the stables," he said, and
he held out his hand to her. They walked out
into the clear morning sunshine.

Flower-bordered paths led around the
side of the house and onto a graveled road
to the fenced yard in front of the stone stables. There were tubs of bright, spritely
primroses along the fence. Unlatching the
gate so Jess could go through, Peter led her
into the building itself.

From each glossy white horse stall a
graceful equine head emerged. Peter
stopped to speak to a wiry man, who doffed

his cap to bare a grizzled gray head.

"Morning, your lordship," the man greeted Peter.

Startled, Jess realized for the first time Peter had a title.

"Good morning, Frank. This is Miss Baird, one of our guests. I'm showing her around," he told him. Then Peter explained to Jess, "Frank's our head groom and stable manager. In charge of the other lads."

Then, reaching into a barrel of apples, Peter passed some to Jess and took several himself. "My horses always expect a treat," he said, smiling as he led her back to the double row of stalls. "Do you ride?"

"Not well," Jess replied, thinking of the few times she had been on an old horse put out to pasture on a neighbor's farm.

"You'll have to learn," Peter said matter-of-factly, and Jess's heart leaped foolishly. She couldn't help wondering if Peter was planning a possible future for them.

As they went along the row of stalls, Peter stopped to rub the nose of each horse, call it by name, then offer an apple. He told Jess the breeding of each horse, rattling off sires and mares.

"We used to raise racehorses. But it became too costly, too much of a financial risk. They are such delicate creatures and must be brought along for at least two years before they begin to return any of the investment. And even then, only if you have tremendous luck." He paused to murmur some endearment to a particularly handsome horse, black with a white star on its forehead. "How's my sweet Sunshine, today, eh?" He smiled rather sheepishly at Jess. "My favorite mare. Could be a winner. But Uncle and I have had to realize racehorses are a luxury only royalty can indulge in these days."

As they made the rounds of the stable, Jess overcame her initial timidity about feeding one of the horses from her upheld hand and touching the delightful velvety softness of their noses.

Back out into the yard, after Peter had a few more exchanges with Frank, he turned to Jess and asked, "Would you like to go for a spin, take a drive through the estate?"

They walked out the stable yard and a few steps farther to the garage where Peter's shiny red roadster was parked. He opened the passenger door for Jess. As she settled into the creamy leather bucket seat and fastened the safety belt, Peter slid behind the wheel and asked, "Top down all right?"

"Sure!" replied Jess thinking regretfully of

her scarf that had blown away on the Haworth moor.

Peter shifted into reverse, backed out, and spun around. Then with a sputter of gravel they roared down the curving driveway.

Jess uncomfortably discovered Peter drove like a race driver. This was even more unnerving as they sped along the narrow country roads on the left-hand side. She soon relaxed, however, because although Peter drove fast, he controlled the wheel skillfully.

Every once in a while Peter smiled over at her confidently, and Jess decided Peter was probably never happier than when on horseback or behind the wheel of a fast-moving motorcar.

As they drove along Jess felt incredibly happy. She had every reason to be, with the soft spring wind in her face, the warm April sunshine, the beautiful winding valley through which they drove. Honey-colored stone cottages nestled in wooded hollows all along the high-hedged lanes.

This was the England she had longed to see and hoped to find. Then, suddenly she sighted a hillside bright with nodding yellow daffodils. "Oh, look!" she exclaimed in delight, pointing as they went by, "Just like Wordsworth's poem!"

But Peter looked blank, and Jess felt a

little disappointed that he had not connected Wordsworth's lovely "host of golden daffodils" to the reality they had just passed. Maybe Peter didn't read poetry. Jess realized that was no crime, but an annoying little voice reminded her that Graham would have caught it immediately.

They drove along in companionable silence. Conversation was almost impossible over the sound of the powerful motor, and Jess was simply enjoying the scenery of the beautiful, almost unpopulated countryside. Wild ponies frisked on the hilltops, and black-faced sheep grazed the lush meadows with their fluffy lambs frolicking nearby.

It was late afternoon before Peter asked, "Hungry? Shall we stop for tea?"

A little farther along, Peter swerved the car onto a side road, hardly wide enough for a single car and canopied by tall poplars. They came out to a cleared space in front of a grey stone and timber building that looked more like a home than a tea shop.

They parked in a place and at an angle that would have made them a prime target for being towed away in an American town. Then Peter opened Jess's door and helped her out. They walked along past quaint little shops and stores Jess would have liked to explore and right to the inn door which opened right onto the street.

Peter led her into a low-ceilinged, rough-beamed room, with bright covers on comfortable chairs, small tables, and a fire gleaming a welcome in a brick fireplace.

"In the sixteenth century this was a coaching inn, a way station for stagecoaches. It's been in continuous operation since then," Peter told her.

"Not under the same management, I presume!" Jess pretended shock.

Peter laughed. "Scarcely! But the same people have been in charge since I've been coming here, and that's no myth."

Inside, Jess was delighted to see that flowered chintz curtains accented the many-paned windows. There were several small round tables set around the room, and on each one a vase of fresh spring flowers nodded gaily.

"They'll serve you tea or coffee in an earthenware mug with your name on it, if you like," Peter informed Jess as they were seated.

She looked at him skeptically. "Really?"

"Look over there!" he directed, and she turned to see a wall covered with mugs hanging from hooks. Each was painted with a name.

"Jessamyn isn't exactly a common name," she said slowly.

"We'll see," said Peter, and he gave their names to the genial waitress.

Finding a mug marked "Peter" was no problem, but Jess had to settle for "Jessica."

"That's probably the English version of Jessamyn, anyway," she shrugged.

"Is 'Jessamyn' American?" asked Peter.

"Scottish. My grandmother was a Scottish war bride. Luckily, my grandfather's family were originally from Scotland, so her family was not too upset when she married an American flyer stationed in Scotland during World War II."

"And lived happily ever after?"

"I think so. I hope so," Jess replied. "Grandmother Jeanie always seemed cheerful and happy. Of course, she probably missed her family and her native land, but she and my grandfather were a most loving couple." Jess paused. "Of course, she loved everything Scottish. She used to tell my sister and me about her own childhood in Scotland. Then, she kept many of the lovely customs and passed them on to her own children."

"I've heard that often emigrants are more Scottish or British or whatever than the people who remain in their native lands," remarked Peter.

"I think that may be true of the Scots in Canada and America. Probably of the British, too! Like the old story of the Englishmen dressing for dinner in the jungle, right?"

They both laughed.

"And what will be your pleasure today?" they were asked by a plump young waitress with a scrubbed, shiny face, as she rolled a tea trolley over for them to choose from the assortment of delicacies.

"Oh, I don't know! Everything looks scrumptious and terribly fattening!" Jess said, trying to look guilty, as her eyes devoured richly iced walnut cake, tarts glistening with luscious strawberries, and fruit pies shimmering with glaze.

"Surely, that's something you don't have to worry about!" Peter remarked as if shocked.

Finally she made her choice — a lemon cheesecake topped with cherries. She took a bite, closed her eyes in rapture, and sighed, "The way I've been eating on this tour, I don't know. I'll probably have to go on a diet and exercise program when I get back to the States." She sighed again. "But it's been worth it."

"By the way, what will you do when you get home?" Peter asked. "I really don't know very much about you, Jessamyn."

"Do? You mean what kind of work? Or do I go to school or have a job?"

"Yes, that sort of thing," Peter said.

"Actually, I'm unemployed!" Jess gave a little laugh.

"What do you mean?" Peter seemed puzzled.

"I was laid off, fired, just before I came on this trip."

"You mean *sacked?*" Peter looked at her aghast. "Whatever for? It seems you'd be an asset to any employer."

"Thank you, sir, for that vote of confidence." She smiled. "I wasn't let go for any personal reasons. The downtown store where I worked was closing. Too many suburban shopping malls springing up all over the place. People don't like bucking traffic, finding parking places, and fighting crowds when they can shop more easily and conveniently nearer their homes."

"I see," was Peter's response, but Jess felt he did not really understand. She started to explain further but was interrupted by the waitress coming to refill their mugs with fresh tea.

"So you lost your job and decided to take this trip?" Peter asked, picking up their conversation.

"Well, not exactly. You see, before I could decide what to do next, Aunt Mil called and invited me to come with her on this tour."

"So that's it!" Peter said as if a puzzling question had been answered. "You came as your aunt's companion. I couldn't help but wonder why a young person, especially someone so full of life and enthusiasm as you, would choose this tour. I mean, it's made up mostly of middle-aged couples and retired persons. Hardly the kind of tour I would normally think someone our age would select."

"What kind of tour would you have expected me to take?" Jess asked him, amused at his obvious relief at her explanation.

"Oh, one with lots more exciting activities planned. Not simply pilgrimages to authors' birthplaces and old churches and houses." Peter shrugged. "I just can't imagine —"

Peter never finished his thought because he suddenly looked at his wristwatch and exclaimed, "Oh, I say, we'd best get going. We'll just make it back home in time to bathe and change for dinner. The old boy is a stickler for punctuality, so we mustn't be late."

When they got back in the car and Peter turned on the engine, he remarked, "We'd better stop for petrol in the next town."

They had only driven a short distance when Peter took a turnoff, and almost immediately they were driving into a picture-book English village.

Jess sat up straight as Peter shifted the car into low gear and they inched along enchanting little streets bordered by thatched-roof cottages set in gardens of bright flowers. At the end of the street, its stately tower shadowing all, stood a lovely Gothic church.

"Oh, how quaint! Would you mind if I took a look around while the car's being serviced?" she asked Peter.

"Not at all. We've still got plenty of time," he agreed, although somewhat hesitantly.

Jess scrambled out of the car and started strolling down the sidewalk outside some interesting little shops. At one she stopped to look in the window and saw a fascinating jumble of books, old and new, the kind she knew instinctively Graham would have enjoyed rambling through, too.

In a few minutes Peter followed her and gazed about indifferently. Jess would have loved to go inside all of them to browse and look about, especially the small intriguing bookstore. But she sensed Peter was getting restless. He was probably the kind of man easily bored by endless meandering in and out of shops. So she restrained her own impulse, and soon they were back in the car.

On the way home they joked and sang and were deliciously silly. Jess would always think of that day with Peter as one of sunshine and carefree laughter.

Back at Fortnay Hall they had run up the terrace steps together, hand in hand, laughing at some bit of nonsense when they were met by the butler telling Peter he had a telephone call.

Peter excused himself and went inside. At almost the same time Graham Campbell sauntered out of the house. He stopped when he saw Jess, who was getting her small brush out of her handbag to work on the tangles in her windblown hair. He gave her a long, speculative look and remarked drily, "You look as though you two have been having a good time."

Jess smiled back at him brightly, "Oh, we have! Marvelous!"

Graham's brows drew together in a frown. *What in the world is the matter with him?* Jess thought, annoyed. Didn't he like seeing people have fun? Or could Aunt Mil possibly be right? Was Graham jealous of Peter? Of Peter being interested in *me?*

Just then Graham drew a small package

from his jacket pocket and handed it to her.

"By the way," he said, "here's something for you."

Puzzled, Jess took it, pushed aside the tissue paper in which it was wrapped, and saw it was a square of yellow silk, a scarf almost identical in color and pattern to the one she had lost on the moors.

"Why, thank you, Graham," she said, touched by his thoughtfulness. "That was very nice of you. But you didn't—"

"I wanted to," he interrupted. "Maybe it will change my image. I'm not all bad, you know."

Jess laughed a little self-consciously. "I never said that or thought it either."

"Are you too tired, or would you care to stroll through the topiary maze?" was Graham's next question.

"I'm not too tired," Jess began, "but there's really not much time before dinner. I want to go freshen up—"

"Well, fine, then," Graham interrupted her in a way that implied it was anything *but* fine. He jammed his hands into the pockets of his jacket and went past her without another glance.

"Thanks anyway!" Jess called after him. "See you later."

But Graham neither turned his head nor

responded. Jess wasn't even sure he'd heard her. She shrugged and started into the house. There she met Peter coming out from the library.

"Oh, Jessamyn, good! I was hoping to find you. Look, something unexpected has come up, and I'll have to be away tomorrow."

Peter was frowning and seemed ill at ease.

"Is anything wrong?" Jess asked.

"Wrong?" he repeated. "No, nothing's wrong. Just a muddle. See here, Jessamyn, there's something I really ought to tell you." Peter seemed hesitant.

"So tell me!" she said teasingly, but she felt a vague uneasiness.

"Let's go in here where we can talk privately," Peter suggested. He took Jess by the arm and led her into the glassed conservatory. It had been added when a Victorian Fortnay wife, who had been raised in India where her father was a British officer, longed to grow familiar exotic flowers and plants.

In a bower at one end were a set of white iron lace chairs, a bench, and a table. The moist air was heavy with fragrance as Peter seated Jess and took a place beside her.

"That phone call just now was from Hilary Holmes, the girl I was engaged to until last November," he said, never taking his eyes off Jess's face.

"Engaged?" she repeated blankly. She felt a sudden churning in the pit of her stomach.

Peter nodded. Pressing his lips together tightly, he waited a moment longer before continuing.

"Hilary and I have known each other for ages. We used to see each other when we were both home from boarding schools at Christmas and in the summers. We did the ordinary things — played tennis, swam, rode. We were jolly good comrades, actually, until —" he paused. "It's hard to explain just how it happened, being engaged, I mean."

Peter seemed distracted. "I'm not sure you'd understand," he said slowly.

"Try me," urged Jess, wondering what was coming next.

"Right. Well, then when she came out, made her debut, had her London season, I was, naturally, one of her escorts. It simply began to be taken for granted that we — people assumed — after all, we'd practically grown up in the same nursery!"

"You got engaged," prompted Jess.

"That's about the size of it. But last fall we had a huge quarrel." Peter shook his head, smiling slightly. "I'm not quite sure what it was about now, but it was hot. We both said a lot of things and the result was, we broke it off. Our engagement, I mean. Hilary went off to the Continent — to France and Italy. I think she visited some girlfriend she'd had at school or something. Lives in a villa in Capri, I think. Anyway, she's come back. She wants to see me," Peter said flatly. He was still watching Jess for her reaction.

"When?" Jess asked.

"Right away. Tomorrow."

"She lives nearby?"

"A short distance."

"And?"

"I said I'd come. She said there was something important we had to discuss. I can't think what." Peter looked dismayed. Then suddenly he began to laugh.

"What is it? What's so funny?" asked Jess.

"I just thought of what it might be," he chuckled.

"What, Peter?" begged Jess, painfully curious.

"I believe she went off with the ring I gave her! It was a family heirloom. Oh, not terribly valuable in itself but a traditional thing. A citrine in a cluster of small diamonds in a gold setting." He looked thoughtful. "I suppose that's it. But — she could have sent that back by mail. It must be something besides that."

They were silent for a few minutes. Jess studied a beautiful spray of cymbidium orchids. It was Peter who broke the silence. He took both of her hands in his and held them tightly.

Looking regretful he told her, "I want you to know that what I said to you last night is true. I meant every word of it. I do think I'm falling in love with you, Jessamyn. I haven't given Hilary much thought for weeks — months, really. And I haven't thought of her at all since meeting you. You do believe me, don't you? I'd never have said anything to you if I had felt in any way engaged to someone else!"

"Of course, Peter, I believe you."

He raised her hands to his lips and kissed her fingertips. "Good! I would hate it awfully if you thought I was some kind of a—"

"I don't, Peter. I wouldn't ever. I think you're —" Jess stopped herself in time before she blurted out "marvelous." Instead she said, "I think you're a true gentleman."

"And I think you're a love," he said, smiling.

They sat looking at each other for another minute. Then Peter said, "So there it is. There's nothing for it but to go over to see her and get it over with. I rather dread postmortems." Peter sighed resignedly.

"Well, maybe she just wants to show you her color slides of Italy!" said Jess with a mischievous twinkle.

Peter laughed, "Oh, you *are* delicious! You really are a delightful girl, Jessamyn. An extraordinary girl!"

He stood and pulled her to her feet, then circled her waist with his arm, and they started walking slowly out of the conservatory.

"When will you go?" Jess asked.

"In the morning, first thing," Peter replied. "It's really too bad. I had plans for us for tomorrow."

"Well, there's still this evening," Jess said cheerfully. "We have all evening."

As it turned out they didn't. A chance remark of Aunt Mil's led Colonel Fortnay to approach Jess right after dinner and to monopolize her for the rest of the evening.

"Young lady, your aunt tells me you're interested in doing some brass rubbings," he confronted her. "Did you know we have an original Carolean chapel on the place with some truly fine brasses? Since this is a private estate they are not badly worn. In fact, they are in very good condition."

"Actually, I've never done any and don't know too much about it," Jess protested mildly. She almost wished she had never mentioned to Aunt Mil what Esther Whitley had suggested she do while in England. Regretfully now she remembered Esther's saying, "They make excellent wall hangings and can be used in many decorative ways, as table tops, box covers, screens! People love them. You could probably sell them for good prices. If you bring them in to me, I can tell you where to get them framed or sell them to one of my clients for you."

With Jess's admission that she knew nothing about the art, Colonel Fortnay proceeded to educate her. He took her into the library and brought out thick books of pictures of some of the most famous effigies. He recounted at length the life histories of the famous and infamous deceased whose remains were elaborately buried under elegant brass effigies.

Peter came to the door several times during the course of the evening and signaled Jess despairingly. But there was no stopping the Colonel once he was launched into a favorite topic. There was no escape for Jess.

Anyway, in spite of wanting to be with Peter, she did find the subject fascinating. Since Peter would be gone the next day anyhow, it would be an interesting and maybe profitable way to spend the day.

By the time Jess was free, Peter had been pressed into playing bridge. She gave him a wan wave and nod. Then, sleepy from the long, eventful day, she went upstairs to bed.

Chapter
Eleven

Jess dug into her luggage to locate the brass rubbing paper, tape, and heelball wax she had bought at an art supply store before leaving home. Then she pulled on jeans and a warm sweater and went down to breakfast.

Colonel Fortnay could hardly wait for Jess to finish eating. He was eager to take her out to see the ancestral brasses in the family chapel. So foregoing a second cup of coffee, Jess set out with him on the short walk from the house to the gray stone, ivy-covered chapel.

The chapel had been reverently designed in the shape of a double cross which provided ells for the placement of several marble statues. There were others on the altar steps and above the small choir loft. The family members with the most prestige and fame were pictured and buried in the most prominent places. Colonel Fortnay also pointed out the black sheep of the family, memorialized by simple engraved stone flags in the floor.

Beautiful windows under the Gothic stone arches were inset with stained glass coats of arms heralding the family power. Behind the altar a soaring window in the shape of a triple-arch represented the Trinity. Through it a subdued Jessamyn could see a lovely sweep of lawn and ancient trees outside.

She was reminded suddenly of Thomas Gray's "Elegy Written in a Country Churchyard." No doubt the Fortnays buried here were wealthier than Gray's simple folks, but all had shared "the knell of parting day."

As she stepped inside the dim interior she did so with a sense of awe. In this small place there was a feeling of the three centuries of family life and Christian faith expressed in the Gothic forms that surrounded them. Jess felt rather astounded when she saw the statues of men and women who had lived in the manor house and come here to worship, to have their children christened, and to be buried.

Patches of morning light tinted by stained glass lent a sense of timelessness, and yet the presence of the dead all around and under her feet reminded her of the fleeting passage of life. Their footsteps echoed on the stone flags as they walked between the crypts under the floor. Colonel Fortnay's voice echoed, too, as he gave Jess bits and pieces of the history of his ancestors. Jess was struck by the brief lives most of them had had in the light of modern man's longevity. Two of the raised statues portrayed young mothers with their babies in their arms, a reminder that only a few generations ago, childbearing too often had been an occasion for mourning rather than joy.

"Now, I think you have everything you need, my dear," Colonel Fortnay said. "Now I'll leave you to your work."

When he had bustled out, the little chapel rang with silence. The quiet was uneasy as Jess settled herself, but she became accustomed to the stillness, the aloneness of being there. Gradually a peace seemed to filter through to her and the slight eeriness diminished. She walked around again, her crepe-soled shoes making a slight squeak on the stone floors, as she tried to decide which brass she would do first.

What stories lie behind all these? she thought, intrigued as she examined Lady Elinore Fortnay, elegantly attired in a draped mantle and jeweled necklace, her headdress the fashionable "butterfly" style with hair brushed over wire wings, then veiled.

Lord Robert, her husband, beside her, was depicted in cuirass and breastplate, broadsword clasped in his hands, as befit his role in the English Civil War. On the touching small effigy of their son, Edward, his pet dog was etched as a footstool. All these were once real people, living in the house where Jess had slept last night! They had talked, laughed, loved, and wept on the very grounds where she had walked that morning! History was very much with her as she set to work.

Jess decided to start with this couple who somehow appealed to her romantic imagination, and who seemed to have had a sadly tragic story. From the dates it would appear Sir Robert had come home from fighting for the king to find his young wife and child both had died in his absence.

She kneeled on a cushion on the floor and dusted the brass of Lady Elinore carefully with a chamois cloth, removing grit from the crevices with a long-bristled brush. When no dirt appeared on a clean soft cloth run over the effigy, Jess was ready to lay the rubbing paper over the entire figure. She rolled the wide paper out, taping it firmly along the edges so that it would not slip once she began rubbing. Then Jess took her heelball wax and began working downward from the top of the figure. It was hard work, and she could hear herself breathe harder as she rubbed vigorously. Periodically she would stop, sit back, and take a long breath. Then she would slide the pillow farther down, take her position again, and go back to work.

Once she got the knack of it, as Esther Whitley had rightly predicted, all it took was plenty of elbow grease.

While her hands were busy, Jess's mind wandered freely. So many thoughts floated randomly, until gradually they began to take shape. She thought particularly of her day with Peter. How charming he was, how easy to be with. An uncomplicated, lighthearted fellow — or was it lightweight? The sudden impression of him struck. Peter had not made a single comment or remark or suggestion yesterday that could possibly be construed as original, thought provoking, or, for that matter, important! Jess realized she had been totally relaxed. Certainly it had been entirely different from the time she spent with Graham when they were inadvertently left behind in Haworth.

Every time she had been with Graham she had been challenged, confronted, made to defend an idea or opinion — made to think! With Peter, there was no tension, none of that emotional seesaw she felt around Graham.

Funny, but Peter reminded her in a way of a surfer she had met one summer at a beach resort where her family had vacationed. Jess couldn't even remember his name right now, but he had been bronzed and muscular, with sun-streaked fair hair. Beautiful but brainless. Because all the other girls were swooning over him and he had asked Jess to go out, she had dated him all summer.

They had played at love, she and that sun-burned Adonis, lightly, gaily, sweetly. Then at the end of the summer they had said good-bye, and it was over.

A summer romance! she thought. *Probably like a shipboard romance or —*

Whatever conclusion Jess had been about to make was blown right out of her mind by a gust of fresh air as the chapel door was pushed open.

Startled, she jerked her head around and saw in amazement Graham Campbell standing there holding a covered wicker basket.

"What are you doing here?" she demanded.

"I've brought you tea. Well, actually, much

more than that. The English provide very well for what they call their 'elevenses.' It's halfway between an American picnic and an English lunch, I'd say. At any rate, I've got enough in here for the two of us. Come on, young lady, off your knees and out of this gloomy place and into the sunshine. I bet you don't even know the sun is shining out there, do you?"

She needed his strong hand on her elbow to help her to her feet. She realized she was stiff from maintaining the same crouching position for some time.

"Well, thank you very much." She paused, feeling a bit awkward that it was Graham Campbell, of all people. "How did you know I was down here?" she asked rather shyly.

He grinned. "Well, my old Scottish grandmother always told me I'd find the nicest girls in church. So I decided I'd take a look! And here one is!"

Jess had to laugh. She followed him as he led the way down the small nave and out another arched door into the bright sunshine of the April day. She blinked after the dimness in which she had been working all morning.

"Come over here. I've already scouted out a perfect spot."

He had. A gnarled oak tree, newly budded

into leaf, provided a soft, grassy mound underneath its spreading branches. He laid out a car rug for them to sit on and then opened the basket.

He set out a small loaf of thinly sliced; rough-grained brown bread; small containers of butter, mayonnaise, mustard, pickles; generous slices of cheese and ham for sandwiches; along with a thermos of tea and a tin of chocolate-covered cookies, which the English call biscuits.

"My word!" Jess exclaimed. "What a picnic! You must have an 'in' with the cook!"

"More like a cook with an inn!" corrected Graham. "I have to confess. You see when I heard Colonel Fortnay tell someone what you were up to today, I decided touring the Wedgwood factory and museum was not exactly the best way to spend my day. So I left the ladies oohing and ahhing over teacups and table settings, walked out to the road and hitched a ride back to the village in a delivery truck. And then I had this idea and stopped at the inn to have them make up this picnic basket for us."

"It was a lovely idea and I'm grateful. I didn't realize just how hungry I was until now," Jess declared.

They made their sandwiches and drank their tea in mutually satisfactory silence.

Both enjoyed the light breeze rustling the fresh green leaves above them, the warmth of the spring sunshine, the pale green aura that seemed delicately to touch everything about them.

It's an idyllic setting. Jess thought with pleasure. *England in April! Nothing could be more perfect,* she sighed.

Graham seemed thoughtful, too, but when he spoke it was not of England but of California.

"I was just thinking how different it is here from where I live. England seems so small, so neat, in comparison to the rugged northwest. The college town where I teach is right on the coast, and I live at the beach about fifteen miles away. It's a rustic house, built of native stone and redwood on a cliff overlooking the ocean. From nearly every window you can have a sweeping view of the Pacific." He paused. "I got it by happenstance. A colleague of mine was going on sabbatical and wanted someone to live there, take care of the place while he was away. I'd been out there enough times to know what it was like and was glad to volunteer for the job." He laughed and shook his head, then said, "Rough duty, but then someone had to do it!"

"But then he came back?"

"No, what happened was — well, it's the kind of romantic thing you'll really like!" Graham told her with a twinkle in his keen blue eyes. "He was touring the Greek Isles and met a lovely lady who also happened to be the daughter of some millionaire shipping tycoon. In short order they got married. I understand they had an authentic Greek wedding, and now they're living on one of those islands, probably one she owns!" he laughed. "And I got his house!"

"That's quite a story!" Jess conceded.

"It's true," Graham repeated.

"I believe you," she told him.

"I believe you'd believe just about anything romantic," Graham said softly, holding Jess in a steady thoughtful gaze. "I just hope —" he stopped as if about to say something more and then decided against it.

"You just hope — what?" Jess demanded.

"That your romantic longings don't get you hurt."

"I don't know what you mean."

"Don't you, Jess? Don't you really?"

Jess felt faintly wary. She did not really want to hear what Graham was thinking, and yet she resented his assumptions about her. The subject was getting too personal, and making her uncomfortable.

Jess got to her feet, saying, "I really should

170

get back to work. It was a wonderful break. Thank you very much for the picnic. My energy's restored. In fact, I even feel strong enough to help clean up before I go back to vigorous rubbing!" She raised her arm as though showing muscle.

"Would it bother you if I watched?" Graham asked, also getting up, helping her to stow away the remains of the food into the basket.

"No, but you'd probably find it boring just to watch."

"I don't think so. Boredom depends on the company."

He swung the basket up and matched his long stride to her shorter one as they started walking back toward the chapel.

In the chapel Jess laid out her materials for going back to the rubbing of Lady Elinore Fortnay for whom she was beginning to feel a real affection.

Imagine! Jess thought, *Married at fourteen, dead five years later, and such a pretty, dainty, elaborately dressed lady she was. At least in death!*

About ready to start work again, Jess suddenly became conscious of Graham's restless presence. He was pacing back and forth behind her and in such a small space Jess knew she could never concentrate. With a small sigh of exasperation, she looked at him and asked, "Graham, is there something wrong or are you just bored? I warned you this would not be much fun for you."

He stopped pacing, stared at her for a second, then said brusquely, "Well, I do have something on my mind, and I'm trying to decide whether to broach the subject to you."

"You've never held your opinions to yourself before, Graham, so why should you do it now? Tell me what you're thinking."

"All right, I will. I think you've gone all moonbeams and magic about Fortnay Hall, and you see Peter as a young Lochinvar, the White Knight, the heir apparent, or whatever you want to call him. I think you're dreaming that this is all real and that maybe, just maybe, the prince will offer the glass slipper to the little tourist from America and she will step into the throne room and all will live happily ever after."

Indignation sent little flames of color into her cheeks. Her eyes flashed and she opened her mouth to retort when Graham held up his hand warningly,

"Now, before you explode, you asked me, remember? I'm just telling you what I think. But what you ought to know, Jess, is what I've found out."

Jess's hands were clenched into tight little fists.

"And just what is that?" she asked coldly.

"First, let me ask you a question. Does Peter know your aunt won this trip for herself and you as her guest?"

"Just what are you implying?"

"That Colonel Fortnay's nephew's interest in you could be prompted by the fact that he thinks you are a rich American debutante, idling away a few 'thou' to accompany her aunt on this tour." Graham paused significantly. "The fact that you happen to be attractive, charming, and delightful are all bonuses. What more could an impoverished English gentleman ask for than a wealthy wife with quantities of U.S. dollars?"

"*Impoverished? Peter?*" Jess flung out her hands in an encompassing gesture. "Are you *blind?* With all this? The grounds? The gardens? The gorgeous house with all its tapestries, paintings, artifacts? Museum class antiques worth a fortune? *Impoverished?*" Jess shook her head. "Really, Graham, you've gone too far!"

"It's true, Jess, much as you don't want to believe me. I've made a little private tour of Fortnay Hall, an exploratory one beyond the official bounds and probably not 'good form' and all that sort of upper-class good manners. But I had my doubts that all was as it seemed on the surface. Other families have had to do much the same thing. There's no disgrace in trying to make an honest buck by opening the ancestral home to tours and such. I just didn't want you to be misled into thinking—"

"Who appointed you my private detective?"

"No one. But I had my own reasons. And what I found out is that except for the guest rooms and the ones we see, Fortnay Hall is falling apart, badly in need of repairs of all kinds. Maintaining an estate like this must cost a fortune, and I don't think the Fortnays have that kind of money anymore. Nor do I think the farm produces enough to earn them any kind of real income. The family is desperately short of funds, and unless I miss my guess, the Fortnays will lose this place — that is — *unless* —" Graham stopped for a second as though not sure whether to go on.

Then he said, "Oh, they're keeping a good face on it, the old British stiff upper lip and all that. But it's my understanding that unless young Lord Peter Fortnay marries wealth, Fortnay Hall will go the way so many other old family homes have gone — to the real estate speculators to be split up in small lots, subdivided."

Again Graham stopped to look at Jess for some reaction.

But Jess's first reaction to what he was saying was a shocked silence.

Graham went on, "I think you should know, Jess, young Fortnay thinks you're an American heiress."

"How could he possibly think *that!*" demanded Jess.

"Well, this tour isn't exactly cheap. It costs about three thousand dollars per person. But, one could estimate even more considering the accommodations, the length of the tour, the side trips, all the amenities. I couldn't have afforded it, I know. My original tour cost about half what this one does. It was only because it was the travel agency's mistake and my time in England was limited that they had no alternative but to put me on this one instead."

When Jess still didn't say anything, Graham asked, "So you see how it looks. Anyone on this particular tour must be, to say the least, affluent. Draw your own conclusions as to what Peter assumes."

"You are really incredible! Poking and prying and sneaking about gathering evidence like some cheap private eye! Who asked you to do such a thing? As for your so-called protection, I never asked for nor wanted it! It seems a particularly nasty sort of thing to have done to people who have treated you as a guest! I couldn't care less what you think you've discovered about the Fortnays' finances, but I do resent what you've implied about Peter's interest in me! How dare you assume something like that? What right have you to believe you know other people's motives? Just who do you think you are, anyhow?"

"You're such an innocent, Jess. You need someone to look out for you, to take care of you—"

"Of all the egotistical nonsense!" Jess stared at Graham aghast. "I've been on my own nearly two years. I do *not* need a keeper! I'm disgusted that you would stoop to such tactics, Graham. I had a higher opinion of you than this. Going around behind some-one's back, making up all sorts of stories, I — I —" Jess was so angry she could not find any more words. She began gathering up her things.

Graham looked stricken, "I'm sorry, Jess, I—"

"You're always sorry after you've said or done something! Sorry when it's too late!"

"I thought you ought to know—"

"For my own good?" she snapped. "Thanks a lot!"

"Well, no, maybe, for *mine* . . ." He stepped directly in front of Jess and fixed her with his keen blue eyes. "My timing was probably terrible. But, I was afraid if I—"

"If! If *what?* What possible end has it served for you to say all these terrible things?"

"If it would make you see the truth —"

"The *truth?* I think what you've said about Peter is inexcusable."

"Okay! Maybe I had the wrong motive for telling you. Maybe it's because —" He stopped cold. Then in a swift movement, he put out his arms and pulled Jess to him. Before she could move or protest, Graham's arms pulled her close so strongly her head tilted back. For a long moment those blazing blue eyes were inches from hers. The next thing she knew, his mouth was on hers in an ardent kiss.

His arms wrapped around her, holding her tightly. The kiss was long, and if Jess had not been so angry she might have yielded to its compelling sweetness.

As it was, she put her palms against his chest and pushed back. When he let her go, she was shaky and breathless.

She stared at Graham.

"*That's* your excuse?" she asked scathingly.

"I'm sorry, Jess. I shouldn't have done that, but —"

Jess whirled around, began picking up her paraphernalia, dropping things, making a great clatter, not hearing what Graham was saying.

"Listen, Jess, I'm sorry — It's because I love you —"

"Forget it! I've had enough of your apologies!" she said over her shoulder, as she grabbed up her raincoat and brushed past him, avoiding the arm he put out to stop her. She pushed open the chapel door and let it slam behind her.

Outside the chapel Jess ran over the velvety green lawn toward the house. Somehow the day had lost its radiance. She desperately wished Graham had never come out to find her. His inquisitive probing had ruined everything. She had just begun to think differently about him, to like him! Why had he told her those things about the Fortnays, planted those suspicions about Peter in her mind? It wasn't true. She was sure it wasn't! And yet —

She had just reached the crest of the gentle sloping terraced lawns which swept down to the circular driveway when she saw

Peter's small red roadster, with the top up today, round the bend and come to a stop in front of the house.

Then she saw that he was not alone. Someone was sitting beside him. She watched as Peter got out, ran around to the other side of the car to open the door.

Jess felt a clutch of dismay. Peter hadn't said Hilary would be coming back with him to Fortnay Hall. As she stood there, stunned into immobility, Peter helped a willowy blonde out of his car. Jess thought ruefully of something Aunt Mil said when Jess told her Peter was going to see his ex-fiancée.

"Well, I wouldn't worry a bit," Aunt Mil had said with hearty assurance. "You can withstand any competition. Besides, she's probably a horsey English girl — tall, tweedy, and talking tack room, tracks, and trainers."

Here was a far cry from the competitor Aunt Mil had prophesied. Hilary Holmes was a perfect English rose of a girl. Peter was closing the car door behind Hilary when he saw Jess and waved.

"Hello there, Jessamyn. Come along, I want you to meet Hilary."

Jess came closer. The closer she came, the more perfect Hilary looked. Her skin was the porcelain and pink poets lyricized. Her fair hair shone like newly minted gold in the afternoon sunshine, and fanned back from her oval face to reveal flat delicate ears with tiny lustrous pearls glowing in each lobe. A ruffled blouse collar peeked out from the jacket of her mauve soft tweed suit.

Jess was immediately conscious of her rumpled raincoat, which she had worn and trundled about for the past month, of her windblown hair. Even her lipstick had long since disappeared.

What a contrast Peter must see in us, she thought with sinking heart.

At Peter's introduction Hilary did not hold out her hand to Jess. She simply smiled pleasantly, then stood there, her arm slipped possessively through Peter's, her elegant head slightly tilted to one side as she surveyed Jess.

Jess floundered, talking too fast, saying too much as she told them about the rubbings she had been doing that day.

"And so did you finish up on my ancestors?" Peter asked, amused.

"Not quite. I was — interrupted." Jess thought how Graham would have enjoyed this scene, and she became furious all over again. "But I intend to have another go to-

180

morrow. Now, if you'll excuse me, I'm all grubby. I'll have to go freshen up before dinner," she gasped finally. Quickly she made her escape.

Chapter
Twelve

That night Fortnay Hall glittered and shone. If any poverty lurked behind its gilded edges there certainly was no evidence of it, Jess decided, as she looked around the dining room. It was a picture of Edwardian splendor.

The long table, covered with an exquisite handwoven linen cloth, was set with magnificent china, sparkling crystal, and ornate silver. An elaborate centerpiece, a gleaming epergne spilling out purple grapes the size of plums, was flanked by tall, twin, twisted candelabra with tapers casting a soft, candlelit glow.

Jess surveyed the name cards in small flower-shaped porcelain holders at each place and found herself seated in the middle of the long table. Peter was seated at one end with Hilary to his left and Patricia Hollings to his right. Colonel Fortnay as the host was at the other end, flanked by Aunt Mil and Graham. Everything was perfection. Everything made the statement of enormous wealth, of generations of gracious living.

Graham Campbell has to be wrong! Jess declared indignantly to herself. Nothing seemed further from the truth than that the Fortnays were on the brink of financial disaster! She glanced down the table trying to catch Graham's eye to tell him so scornfully. Couldn't he realize how mistaken he was? A person would have to be blind not to see they were surrounded by affluence.

But Graham was turned away in conversation with Dr. Stavros, and after a full minute Jess gave up. If she had a chance after dinner she was determined to confront him with the flimsiness of his assertions.

The menu duplicated one served when King Edward VII was a guest at Fortnay Hall and it was a culinary masterpiece. As course after course was served Aunt Mil joked, "No wonder His Majesty had a king-sized weight problem!"

All during dinner Jess was piling up arguments to back up her viewpoint against Graham's. Why, he'd only have to look at Colonel Fortnay tonight to know. No one so at ease, so calm, could have the slightest concern about money.

He looked every inch a member of the nobility tonight, she concluded with satisfaction. In formal evening dress he played the role of host to perfection. Patricia Hollings was simpering like a schoolgirl under his courtly attention.

Charm was, no doubt, an inherited Fortnay family trait, Jess decided, amused as she glanced over at Peter who was at the moment beguiling the little Belgian woman, Mrs. Bault.

As her eyes lingered on Peter, Jess suddenly became uncomfortably aware that someone was staring at her, and she turned to see Hilary observing her.

Jess started to smile, but then chilled by the cold gaze of those icy-blue eyes, the tentative gesture froze on her lips.

Jess remembered the little scene she had witnessed earlier when she came down the stairs before dinner. As she reached the bottom of the steps, she saw Hilary and Peter coming out of the conservatory together.

Hilary's cameo profile was uplifted in rapt attention to Peter. Then he said something that made her laugh, and she bent her head slightly to his shoulder. It was an impulsive gesture, casual in itself, yet it had the suggestive intimacy of a kiss. Jess had turned away quickly, feeling like an intruder.

Now, she looked at Hilary, regally beautiful in a stunning off-one-shoulder evening dress of shimmering beaded material. Its vivid blue made her eyes dance like sparkling sapphires. Jess thought how perfectly she fitted this environment, like a jewel in a priceless setting. She belonged. Like Peter! Jess glanced again at him. He was sitting directly underneath one of six imposing portraits of former Lord Fortnays on the wall behind him.

As this impression crystallized in Jess's mind, there was no resentment, no jealousy, just a calm acceptance of what was exactly right. If she herself, in the wildest fantasy, had ever thought she could "put herself in this picture," as the travel agency poster had so boldly invited, she knew now that it would never have worked.

Peter, charming, engaging, delightful as he was, was not the man Jess was looking for, not the kind of man she wanted to spend the rest of her life with — certainly not the man God planned for her. It had been flattering and fun, part of this fanciful interlude, this unreal fairy-tale time. But that was all. Peter would always be a happy memory in an unforgettable experience. To think it was anything else would be foolish.

Peter, however, had seemed uncharacteristically nervous this evening, just a little off his elegant, smooth stride. Although he had flashed his smile toward her, he had spent more time than usual with the other members of the tour during the social hour before dinner, rather than seeking her out as had become his style.

Perhaps he felt somewhat uncomfortable about Hilary's presence. She had stayed close beside him, following him whenever he wandered a few feet away, slipping her arm through his possessively. It seemed to Jess that Hilary's manner was making an unmistakable statement.

In a way, Jess felt sorry for her. If she was being that obvious she must feel insecure about Peter. Jess wished somehow she could reassure her that she no longer had designs on Peter. But Hilary kept her distance, avoiding any contact with Jess. There was no opportunity to put the other young woman's mind at rest.

After dinner when they went into the drawing room, there was no chance for a private conversation with anyone — Peter, Hilary, or even Graham for that matter — because Colonel Fortnay announced he was showing slides of his most recent expedition to the Himalayas.

With no choice, they all settled down in the comfortable chairs and sofas, while Peter helped his uncle set up the screen and dimmed the lamps.

The show lasted at least an hour and a half. Afterward servants served coffee, cakes, ices, and drinks.

Suddenly Jess felt very tired. It had been a long day. The upsetting scene with Graham Campbell still troubled Jess, and the evening itself, with all its undercurrents, had been stressful.

She decided to slip quietly out of the room and up to bed. Almost unnoticed she went out to the hall and was just starting up the stairs when she heard Peter's voice calling, "Jessamyn, wait!"

She turned, one hand resting on the wide, smooth banister.

Peter strode across the marble floor to her and said with his boyishly apologetic smile, "I'm sorry we haven't had a minute all evening. Did you have a good time? Every time I looked over at you, you seemed to be enjoying yourself enormously. I didn't mean to neglect you."

"I didn't feel neglected. I had a marvelous time. Now I've had a taste of how the other half lives!"

"Or at least how they lived in the 1880s!" Peter laughed.

He reached for her hand, held it a minute, and said, "I'm driving Hilary home tomorrow, but I want to have a talk with you before I go. Sometime before lunch, all right?"

"Of course, Peter."

"Good. Until then, sleep well, Jessamyn. Good night." Peter bowed slightly and raised her hand to his lips.

At that moment, over Peter's shoulder, Jess saw Graham Campbell standing at the drawing room door. His expression — the clenched jaw, the compressed lips, the penetrating look — stunned her. It startled Jess so much she almost called to him to explain, . . .

Explain what, she wasn't sure. But of course, there was no chance. With one rapier-sharp look, Graham turned around and walked stiffly back into the drawing room.

Upstairs in her bedroom, Jess stood at the casement and looked out at the beautiful grounds of Fortnay Hall bathed in moonlight. The sculptured topiary maze, the crescent-shaped stone steps of the terrace leading out to the gardens seemed like a painting, lovely, but remote — an artist's rendition of reality. In her own way she had painted a picture of life at Fortnay Hall, life with Peter, with the dreamlike strokes of imagination. It had nothing to do with real life.

The next morning Jess was up early, and while the others were at breakfast, she slipped out a side door and went out to the chapel. She wanted to finish her interrupted brass rubbing of Lady Elinore.

She unlocked the door with the key Colonel Fortnay had given her and stepped inside. The stone walls and floors felt damp, and deathly cold after being closed all night. She moved stiffly to find the place where she had been when Graham had brought her tea the day before and they had gone to sit out in the sunshine together. What had started out to be delightful had ended disastrously, she remembered ruefully. Why could Graham never leave well enough alone? What was it he said? "There's too much at stake not to be honest. There's too much to lose not to tell the truth."

So? His version of the truth might not be the whole truth. But once something is pointed out it's hard not to look at it in a new light. Even last evening Jess found herself noticing things she had not seen before. Particularly about Peter. Had he really been too busy assisting his uncle with the slide show to find a moment to talk to her? Or was he so confused about his relationship with Hilary that he was avoiding her? Try as she might, Jess had not been able to see if Hilary was wearing the ancestral citrine engagement ring.

Jess put down the small kneeling cushion and got out her materials. She had been concentrating fully for about twenty minutes when she heard the chapel door creak as it swung open behind her. A shaft of light threw a banner of sun across the mount. Jess sat back on her heels, turned her head to see who had come in. To her surprise, it was Hilary Holmes.

Hilary looked every bit as stunning in riding clothes as in an evening gown. Her bright hair was drawn back, and a flat black velvet ribbon was tied at the nape of her neck below the smart little black derby. Her slender figure was graceful in the tailored black broadcloth jacket, faun-colored breeches, and polished leather boots. A creamy silk stock was folded and pinned with a gold bar at her throat.

Her wide blue eyes swept over Jess and took a silent inventory, "I would like very much to talk to you, Miss Baird," she began with a tiny tremor in her distinct, cultured voice betraying a slight nervousness.

"Why, of course." Jess rose from her knees. "But, please, do call me Jess or Jessamyn. Miss Baird seems awfully formal."

Hilary cleared her throat and slapped the small leather riding crop she carried into the palm of one hand as if the gesture provided some assurance.

"I'll be quite frank with you, Miss Baird — Jessamyn. I understand Americans appreciate honesty, and though what I have to say is quite difficult for me, I shall just have to try." Hilary paused and her flawless complexion suddenly flushed pink.

"I can see Peter is quite taken with you. I mean, you're different. You're something quite new to him, and he's attracted. But, I made a terrible mistake of letting Peter go last fall, and I don't mean to make the same mistake again. I mean to get Peter back."

Before Jess could say anything Hilary rushed on, "You see, I've been in love with Peter forever. I always hoped, planned that when we grew up we'd fall in love or rather that he would fall in love with me and we'd marry. I've dreamed about it ever since I was a little girl. I had his picture with me at boarding school and lived for the holidays

191

when I'd come home and get to see him, ride with him, be with him. We began to see each other after my London debut. It was all turning out just as I'd planned. I kept waiting for him to propose, to set the date. When he finally did and gave me the Fortnay ring, I was ecstatic!

"Then, it all fell apart! A stupid quarrel. I made too much of a silly incident and — oh, well, the reasons don't make all that much difference now. We broke up, and I went off to the Continent in a huff! I regretted leaving almost as soon as I was across the channel.

"I just couldn't believe I'd been such a fool!" Hilary exclaimed, giving her poor little palm several sharp slaps with the crop. "Well, when I came back, I found Peter was off on some kind of long tour for his uncle. The tour you're taking! So I just had to bide my time until he got to Fortnay Hall. The minute I heard he was home, I rang him immediately."

"When I got over here, it didn't take me long to see how the land lay. I could tell Peter was interested in someone else. And when I saw you — well, I knew I had to do something right away."

Jess tried to interrupt Hilary, but the girl held up a restraining hand and started pacing back and forth in the small space of the chapel.

Then she turned, and facing Jess directly, she said, "I have an idea you're an idealist. Most Americans are. You have some sort of glamourized version of what Peter is like. Well, I can tell you since I've known him all my life. I know his faults, his flaws, as well as his good qualities. I understand them and him.

"Peter has very expensive tastes. He's in debt to his tailor, his trainer, his auto-mechanic! He's mad about horses and cars and good clothes! All those things are important to someone like Peter."

Hilary paused significantly. "I can afford Peter. I don't think you can. Father has made tons of money in iron ore and all sorts of subsidiary investments. He's a self-made millionaire. I have a yearly allowance that will double when I'm twenty-one. I can give Peter the kind of life he wants to live.

"He may be mildly infatuated with you, and you're probably dazzled by his charm, good looks, this house, and all it seems to stand for. Peter's ancestors, who go back to the Plantagenets, are impressive. But in the end, I think Peter will choose me and the life he's always known — a life I can assure him."

She stopped momentarily, as if out of breath, then added, "I'm willing to wait until his little fling with you is over, but I just thought I should give you fair warning, I think I hold most of the cards, and I intend to play them."

"But, Hilary, I'm no threat to you. I'm not in love with Peter, and he most certainly is not in love with me," Jess said quietly.

Hilary looked startled. "Well, I must say, you're being an awfully good sport about it."

Jess just smiled.

Two hours later Jess, rolling her rubbings carefully, left and locked the chapel door behind her. She met Peter coming toward her along the flower-bordered path.

"All completed?" he asked.

"Just finished doing one of your ancestors and his *three* wives! I must say, Peter, some of the former lords of Fortnay Hall went through wives in a hurry, three in less than eleven years!" she replied teasingly.

"Ah, yes, stout fellows. But one can hardly say the same for their spouses, I suppose. But then there was plague and that sort of thing that finished them off, too. So you mustn't put all the blame on the Fortnays," he responded in the same joking manner.

He fell into step beside her, and they walked along silently for a few minutes.

Then Peter broke the silence by saying, "I'm driving Hilary home after lunch, and I think you should know something, Jessamyn," he began.

He put a hand on Jess's arm and halted her at the crest of the slope exactly where she had stopped the day before when she saw Peter and Hilary drive up.

"I hope I haven't given you the wrong impression, Jessamyn. I do absolutely adore you. I think you're utterly smashing, and I can't think of anything I'd rather do than have what you Americans call a romantic fling, I suppose. But I care too much about you for something like that. Besides, I can tell you're the kind of girl who would expect much more of any relationship than a casual interlude."

Jess felt a smile tug at the corners of her mouth. Peter was having a struggle with this, and it amused her not to help him. She wanted to see that fabulous poise and charm at work.

"You see, I realize I wouldn't be right for you anyway. I think I knew that very soon after I began to get to know you. You're far too bright and interested in all sorts of things I don't give tuppence for — books, music, even travel. I don't really care much for that.

"I love it *here!* England, Fortnay Hall! This is the world I'm really comfortable in."

Peter made a sweeping gesture with his hand to include the river, the garden, and the meadows beyond the manicured lawns. "I was born and brought up here. This is all I really care about, can you understand that? I'd probably bore you to death after a while." He smiled ruefully and let that sink in for a moment before he went further.

"About Hilary — you see she accepts me just the way I am. She neither expects nor wants anything more than I am. We both love the land, riding, horses, and quite frankly, she can help me keep all this — all the things I love.

"It may sound downright materialistic to you, romantic soul that you are, Jessamyn. But for all the glamour of it, what it comes down to is this legendary mansion and the estate require cold, hard cash to run. I must make a very practical decision about marriage. Fortunately, Hilary is beautiful, good-humored, and clear-sighted enough to understand the facts. We are quite compatible. Great comrades, actually. If things were different . . ." Peter gave Jess that smile that she now knew was carefully cultivated to cast its persuasive spell. "I wish I could afford you."

196

Jess stood looking at Peter as he walked away, surprised that she felt nothing more than a sense of release. She hoped he and Hilary would be happy together. There was no question that Peter belonged here at Fortnay Hall with someone like Hilary to complete the picture.

For some reason, then, Jess turned around and returned to the little chapel. She set down her things at the back and slipped into one of the angled alcoves and onto a wooden kneeling bench within it.

The afternoon sunlight began to slant through the triple-arched stained glass windows over the altar, accentuating the dimness of the rest of the interior. As she knelt there a strange, inexplicable quietness seemed to suffuse her. It was a peace, a calm at her very center, that she had never experienced before.

The peace of God, that surpasseth understanding, she thought with awe.

She saw everything with a new clarity. She saw the truth about herself, about Peter — how she had romanticized fantasy into fact. She also saw what Graham had been trying to do and why.

"Ye shall know the truth, and the truth shall make you free."

Jess suddenly felt free.

The tiny ache Jess felt at the bottom of her heart she slowly realized was not for Peter or what might have been between them, but for herself having let Graham believe otherwise.

I must go and find him, she decided. She hadn't liked the way he'd gone about trying to protect her but he had meant well, basically. She owed him that at least.

She got up from her knees, picked up her things, and hurried out into the sunlight.

Jess came into the house and stood uncertainly for a minute in the entrance hall. Where would Graham be? The library? The gallery? Then she heard voices drifting out from the drawing room, the clink of teacups and light laughter, and realized it was tea time. Graham would probably be in there with the others.

She put her things down on one of the Queen Anne chairs beside the hall table. After a quick check of her appearance in the gold-framed mirror above it, Jess walked into the drawing room.

A quick glance around told her immediately Graham was not among the guests. Assuming a purposely casual interest Jess asked nonchalantly if anyone had seen Graham.

"I haven't seen him since breakfast," Emily said.

"Mr. Campbell?" repeated Patricia Hollings overhearing the inquiry. "Oh, he left this morning."

"Left?" echoed Jess blankly.

Patricia shrugged indifferently. "Said he was going fishing!"

"Fishing?" Jess knew she was beginning to sound like an echo chamber.

"That's what he said," Patricia told her, loftily adding, "Strange man leaving before the end of the tour. Ah, well, I never felt he was really one of us! He was always so — so argumentative!"

"Oh, that was just his style. Gruff on the outside, a real Teddy bear inside," laughed Yvonne. "I've known plenty of Texas men just like him," she added as though paying the absent Graham the highest possible compliment.

"Just a man of independent thought." Surprisingly it was Aunt Mil joining Yvonne in Graham's defense. "Intelligence and integrity — a good combination."

"He was a man after my own heart," agreed Yvonne.

Jess turned away and walked over to the window as if to look out at the garden.

Her hands gripped the sides of her teacup to keep it from shaking in her trembling hands. She drank her tea slowly. It was very hot, sweet, and strong. Just what she needed to bolster her against the shock of Graham's departure.

Jess remembered when she had poured out the whole "sorry mess" of her quarrel about Peter and Graham in the chapel, how Aunt Mil had shaken her head and said sadly, "What a rash, reckless fellow he is!" She sighed.

"Surely you don't feel sorry for *him*, Auntie!" demanded Jess, shocked.

"Sometimes people do the wrong things for the right reasons or vice versa. The man's daft over *you*, Jess, and it's propelled him into uncharacteristic behavior, that's all. He tried the desperate ploy of disenchanting you with his rival! And it backfired. Now, he's worse off than he was before. I'm sure he's suffering for it without any help from anyone," Aunt Mil told her firmly.

Her aunt's words echoed in Jess's mind. Graham in *love* with her? *A funny way of showing it*, she thought. And yet, rather typical of him. Blunt, outspoken, awkward. Nothing subtle about him. The truth is what's important, he had said. Too much at stake not to —

The look she had seen on Graham's face last night, when Peter had raised her hand to his lips and kissed it, flashed back into Jess's mind. She saw it now as Graham might have interpreted it. Two lovers bidding each other a tender good night.

Of course, Graham had gone away believing she and Peter —

Feeling vulnerable and unsure of her emotions, Jess put down her teacup and hurried out of the room and upstairs.

When she reached her bedroom, she found Emma, the maid, at the door with the clean laundry.

"Will there be anything else, Miss, you'll be needing? Shall I lay out your dress for the evening?" she asked.

"No, thank you, Emma. I haven't decided what to wear yet," Jess replied, knowing it really didn't matter since no one would be there to care.

The maid started to leave, then turned back saying, "Oh, Miss, I forgot. There's a package for you. Mr. Campbell asked me to place it in your room before he left this morning. It's there on the desk."

Jess's fingers fumbled with the string as she tore off the wrappings. Perhaps Graham had left her some message after all. But all that was inside was a slim volume of poetry. Robert Burns! There was a folded slip of paper sticking out as if marking a page. Quickly Jess turned to it. The poem there was "A Red, Red Rose," and the paper contained a brief note in a bold slanting hand.

Dear Jess,
I know you didn't want any more apologies from me, but here's one last one. I am truly sorry I misrepresented Peter or hurt you. Believe that I wish you every happiness. It will always give me enormous joy to think of you.

Yours
Graham Campbell.

Reading it brought a lump to Jess's throat. But even as she searched it thoroughly there was not another line with an address where Graham could be reached.

Jess doubted if anyone else noticed her distress, except maybe Aunt Mil, who gave her several sharp looks during the gaiety of the party before dinner that evening. Since her unhappiness was her own fault, Jess felt she had no right to inflict it on anyone else, and she tried her best to participate as much as possible in the fun of the last night at Fortnay Hall. They would be leaving the next day for London, and after four days there they would be departing for their separate flights home. The tour would be breaking up.

Later in the evening Jess sought out Colonel Fortnay to have a private word with him to try to find out why Graham had left so abruptly and, maybe, where she could contact him. Colonel Fortnay's reply only made her feel worse.

"I really can't say, Miss Baird. It seemed a sudden decision. Poor chap, seemed to be quite down about something. All he said to me was that something unexpected had come up and he had to go. Didn't indicate whether he was going back to the States straight away or was going to stay longer in London.

"I was sorry to see him leave. Great fellow, keen mind, analytical."

Listening to Colonel Fortnay's complimentary remarks about Graham, Jess felt a growing sense of loss.

How could she have been so dense, so blind, when it came to Graham? She should have been more perceptive.

She thought of how she and her college roommate used to draw up lists of the qualities they wanted in the men they would someday marry. Jess's had been very specific. First of all, he should be a Christian and have a profession he enjoyed. He must be intelligent, be interested in books, travel, and the outdoors, be sincere and open, have a good sense of humor —

Jess stopped short. Hadn't Graham Campbell had all those qualities, fit all those requirements?

Jess thought back to the very beginning, the first time she had seen Graham, the strange intensity with which their eyes had met, almost as if they recognized each other. That inexplicable quickening of her heart had been present even then.

She thought about all the things that seemed happenstance, his tour being overbooked, his joining theirs, those first little verbal duels, the jabs and thrusts, even as they felt drawn to each other. She remembered, too, those sharp little tugs of will, the quick flaring of temper, the laughter — It was the way most of their squabbles dissolved into laughter that lingered now, in Jess's memories.

She recalled particularly one day when she had chided Graham about being negative, called him a dour Scotsman. He had totally disarmed her with unexpected self-mockery when he lapsed into a broad Scottish burr and quoted Robert Burns, "O wae some Pow'r the giftie gie us. To see oursels as others see us!"

Then he had smiled one of his rare smiles

and said softly, "Ah, Jessamyn Baird, I need someone like you to lighten up my life."

Now Jess realized she needed someone like Graham in *her* life to give it balance. She needed his maturity, strength of character, steadiness, and faith. A man like Graham would challenge her, sharpen her appreciation, force her past romantic gloss to the real essence of things. What a fool she had been not to recognize it.

Then it had all ended in that terrible quarrel and misunderstanding. Now it was too late. Graham was gone. There was no way she could find him and bring him back into her life.

Chapter Thirteen

Jess opened her eyes and for a brief moment wondered where she was. She had awakened in so many different rooms in so many different places during the past few weeks, she could not be quite sure. Then she remembered they were back in London. Her second thought was that Graham was gone.

They were scheduled for a full four days here before she and Aunt Mil flew back to the States. The whole fantastic "dream trip" would be over.

It would have been much easier to go back home and pick up her life again if she had never known Graham Campbell. Somehow she knew that after knowing him no other man would ever quite measure up. What a strange, unhappy sequence of mishaps, mistakes, misunderstandings their brief relationship had been! And it was mostly her fault.

How could she have missed what God was so clearly trying to show her? How could she have been so wrong about so many things?

Was it truly "better to have loved and lost than never to have loved at all"? Jess wasn't at all sure that it was.

She sighed heavily, threw back the covers, and got up. She looked forward to these four days in London at the end of the tour so much. But now she felt a singular lack of enthusiasm.

Enough choices here to boggle the mind, Jess thought, reading over the planned tours and alternatives open to her. That morning a tour of the city was scheduled for all. After that they could make individual plans. Right after breakfast they were herded onto the minibus and whisked off to see Oxford Street, the Marble Arch, Picadilly Circus, Pall Mall, and Buckingham Palace where they watched the pageant of the changing of the guard.

Back at the hotel the discussion at the lunch table was on the afternoon's choices — Westminster Abbey, the Tower of London, or Madame Tussaud's Wax Museum.

Jess was undecided, vacillating between the Tower and Westminster. Finally everyone got up from the table and gathered for their choices, and she found herself with the group for the Tower.

Actually it didn't matter, she thought as she got back on the bus. Her spirits were so low that viewing the dungeons and torture chambers of early political prisoners and the rooms where the "retired" wives of Henry VIII wasted away could not make her feel any gloomier. It was as though she were moving in slow motion, like in a heavy dream or more like a nightmare.

As she stood there in line waiting for the Tower tour to begin, Jess saw something that jolted her — a tall man in a gray raincoat up ahead. Something about the set of his shoulders looked familiar. Could it possibly be Graham? She craned her neck, leaning out to peer at him. Then he turned and Jess felt the clutch of disappointment. No! It wasn't Graham. Of course not! Graham was somewhere over the Atlantic by now or on his way or maybe even back in California! And she did not even know the name of the small college where he taught! Stupid!

Jess dug her hands deeper into the pockets of her own raincoat. She glanced again at the man up the line. How could she have thought he was Graham? He was wearing a tweed slouch-brimmed hat, while Graham never wore a hat of any kind. She could see him now the way he had been that day on the moors, the heavy thatch of rusty red hair, tousled, that strong profile turned into the wind as he watched the moor sheep feeding on the rough grass.

Jess shivered involuntarily, turned up her raincoat, collar against the raw wind, and looked away. Her throat suddenly felt tight and sore. Unconsciously she reached into her pocket and pulled out her scarf to tie around her head.

Her fingers on the silky texture thrust a sharp memory deeply into her heart. Graham had given it to her, in his awkward, offhand way. *Such a thoughtful, sweet gesture,* Jess thought, with a little twisting wrench. How he must have searched trying to find one that matched the one that had blown away that day on Haworth moor.

As she tied it on under her chin Jess knew she would always keep this scrap of silk, until it was in shreds, probably. It was the only thing she had to remember Graham by, except the book of poems. "Oh my luve is like a red, red rose."

She had read it over so often she had it memorized. It was like a plaintive nightingale singing in her heart.

How she wished she had known, realized —
She recalled Graham's kiss in the little

chapel. It had had the same startling effect on her as the very first time she had seen him out the bus window.

But it was too late now.

I must stop thinking about him! she scolded herself. *I'm building my feelings, and possibly his, way out of proportion.*

Jess shifted her position in the line impatiently and looked around her. As she did she saw the sign nearby, LONDON BRASS RUBBING CENTER.

In a split-second decision, Jess told Aunt Mil she thought she would rather spend time over there than "doing" the Tower and that she would meet them either back at the bus or at the hotel later.

Jess recalled her first enthusiasm when the head decorator at Danby's had urged her to make as many rubbings as she could to sell when she came home. Mrs. Whitley would be singularly unimpressed with the number Jess was bringing back.

The four she had done in the little chapel at Fortnay Hall were special. She would not dream of selling them. They were precious memories she would cherish forever. They would always remind her of Graham and that sunny afternoon they had spent together.

Of course, they would also remind her of

their terrible quarrel. But then there were so many things about this trip that would remind her of Graham, there was no use trying to forget.

But at least for the next two hours Jess was totally preoccupied with the fascination of making several good rubbings. There were a myriad of marvelous copies of the memorial plaques laid out on waist-high tables for maximum rubbing convenience. The helpful staff graciously provided Jess with all the necessary materials, the chalk and black paper. They even suggested interesting plaques to rub. Jess chose an endearing and unique one to do, Thomas Chaucer, thought by some to be son of the famous Geoffrey of *The Canterbury Tales*, standing in enormous pointed shoes atop a reclining unicorn.

When she had finished and was leaving the center, she found that the tour minibus had departed from the carpark near the Tower. It was getting dusk and a light rain was gently falling. So Jess did something she had always wanted to do. She signaled into the street and was driven back to the hotel in an authentic cab.

Back at the hotel, Jess was greeted with the marvelous news that Colonel Fortnay had managed to secure seats for the tour at the performance of *The King and I*, the

London company's current revival.

In spite of her heartache, Jess tried to act as excited as the rest, and for a few hours she was able to lose herself in the colorful musical.

But later, back in her hotel room, Jess stood at the window, and all the sadness of regret, of the lost chance to explain to Graham about Peter or to explore her own feelings about him, descended on her in a wave of self-pity.

She tried to shake it but it persisted. *I need to pray,* she told herself firmly.

Turning back into the lighted room, she got out the small Bible she carried in her tote bag. She felt guilty remembering how many mornings on the tour she had raced through her simple daily devotions, eager to be off to the day's adventure. Now she knew the only way she was going to rise above her depressed feelings was to search for the answers the only place she was sure she would find them.

It did not take her long to find what she was looking for in Proverbs. She had heard Grandmother Jeanie quote Proverbs 3:6 often enough. Now Jess read it over slowly, letting the ancient wisdom sink into her heart and mind. "In all thy ways, acknowledge him, and he shall direct thy paths."

Jess had to admit she had done what many Christians do, made her own plans then asked God to bless them!

"Trust in the Lord with all thine heart; and lean not unto thine own understanding."

That's exactly what she *had* done, Jess thought, convicted. She had seen things through her own wishes, her own desires, her own *understanding*. Romanticizing Peter to the extent that it had blinded her to reality, she didn't see the truth that they were not meant for each other. Even if there had not been Hilary, it would never have worked.

Then, she had not recognized the value in Graham, beneath his outward blunt, sometimes tactless manner. How foolish, how shallow!

Lord, help me to learn from this! Jess prayed.

Finally, it was their last night in London. It was the end of the tour. There was to be a gala farewell dinner in the hotel's private dining room for the last night they would all be together.

Jess had just finished dressing, fastening in her earrings, when there was a tap at her door, and Aunt Mil came in.

"I'll be ready in a minute, Auntie, unless

you want to go downstairs on your own."

"No, dear, I'll wait," Aunt Mil replied, settling herself in one of the easy chairs.

Jess had on her "theater suit" of royal blue velveteen. It had a short, fitted jacket and gently flared skirt. With it Jess was wearing the Victorian blouse she had bought on her shopping spree that first day in London. *Weeks ago,* Jess thought, remembering how happy she had been back then at the beginning of the tour.

"You look very pretty tonight, Jessamyn," Aunt Mil told her.

Knowing that there would be no one at the party tonight to whom it would matter, Jess unconsciously sighed. Then she glanced up guiltily and met Aunt Mil's sharp eyes in the mirror of the dressing table.

"I don't like to see you so unhappy, Jessamyn. I brought you along on this trip to make you happy. It seems to have succeeded only in making you very sad," her aunt said crisply.

Jess whirled around to protest, "Oh, no, Aunt Mil, don't think that, please. It's been a wonderful trip. I've enjoyed every minute of it — that is — almost. It's just that —" Her voice wavered.

"It's Graham Campbell, isn't it?" Aunt Mil demanded.

"I don't want to talk about it. It's not important."

"But of course it's important!" Aunt Mil declared. "And we *must* talk about it. You're in love with him, aren't you?"

Jess looked at her aunt hopelessly. "I think so — yes."

"Graham Campbell is a true Scot." Aunt Mil shook her head. "Stubborn and very proud. He went off believing you loved Peter Fortnay, right?"

Jess nodded.

"And you had no chance to explain?"

Again Jess nodded.

In a slight Scottish burr, Aunt Mil quoted Robert Burns softly . . . " 'Had we never met — or never parted — we had never been broken-hearted!' Well, my girl, what can I say?"

Jess came over and gave her aunt a hug.

"Nothing, Auntie. And it's certainly not your fault! I can only blame myself for the way things turned out! Come on, let's go downstairs. The party's probably already started!

Jess managed a bright smile and held out her hand, knowing the least she could do to show her aunt her gratitude was to put aside her own feelings and have a good time. At least, she would *try*.

A gourmet meal was served and many toasts were lifted throughout the gala evening. Each member rose to give tribute to their guide and host, and in turn to every other member of the tour. At the end Colonel Fortnay gave a nice little speech, which Jess guessed he probably gave to all of his tours. However, it made them all feel great when he told them they were the most congenial group he had ever hosted.

At the end of the evening they all formed a circle, crossed hands and with Colonel Fortnay's booming baritone leading, began to sing "Auld Lang Syne." As the last chorus died away there was not, as they say, a dry eye in the house. Jess found it hard to sing above the hard lump in her throat.

At last the inevitable farewells had to be said. The mood of dinner subtly changed as the round of good-byes became quietly melancholy. Their weeks together had transformed a group of strangers into friends. These people would always be irrevocably linked with England and the magic of this very special time.

When the last address had been exchanged, the promises to write or visit or call exacted, they all said good night and headed for their own suites.

After Jess had washed up and brushed her

teeth and her hair, she put on her robe and slippers and went into Aunt Mil's room to say good night.

Jess tried to sound cheerful as she said, "Well, Auntie, tomorrow it's Heathrow and home!"

Aunt Mil was already in bed, propped up against pillows, looking at some travel folders. She glanced up as Jess came in and sat down at the foot of her bed. Then she gave her niece a long, speculative look and asked, "What would you think if we extended our trip a few weeks?"

Jess's eyes widened.

"To where, Aunt Mil?"

"To Scotland. I think it would be too bad if we went back home without seeing the land of our ancestors when we're so close. I've always wanted to go, especially to the island of Skye. So what do you think? Are you anxious to get home or shall we go north to Scotland?"

There was only a moment's pause. What, after all, did Jess have to go home to? Job hunting, long, lonely days and nights of regret over Graham? Scotland seemed a far better prospect.

"That would be wonderful, Aunt Mil!"

"Good!" her aunt said briskly. "We'll make our reservations tomorrow and we'll go."

"By the way, Auntie, what's so special about Skye?" Jess asked curiously.

"Why, that's where Flora Macdonald took Bonnie Prince Charlie to help him escape from the British Army. Disguised him as her maid, Betty Burke. We're descended from her, you know. In 1774 she and her husband came to North Carolina and were involved in the American Revolution."

"I do remember Grandmother Jeanie talking about her." Jess nodded her head slowly.

"Mother had a little picture of her, framed with some sprigs of dried heather," Aunt Mil said. "I think it would please her very much if we visit Flora's Skye."

Jess tried valiantly to enter into Aunt Mil's enthusiastic plans for their trip to Scotland. It wasn't fair to burden her aunt with her own unhappiness, especially when she knew she was part of the reason Aunt Mil was extending their tour.

The very next morning Aunt Mil went right out and found a travel agency to plan the best kind of tour for them. She brought back a bundle of beautiful color folders describing various tours through Scotland.

She and Jess spread them out on the bed and started looking through them. As they did Jess began to feel excitement rise, dislodging some of the dull ache that had held her.

In spite of what had happened, Jess knew that a chance like this might never come again, and she was determined to make the most of it.

Sifting through the brochures Aunt Mil began to outline their plans.

"I think a train tour might be the way to see the country better," she said. "We'll go to Edinburgh, of course, and see several historic sites. We'll do some shopping there. I want to stock up on some good sweaters for gifts, and we're both going to get authentic Macdonald tartans and all that goes with a woman's formal clan attire. Then we'll wow 'em at the next Robert Burns birthday celebration at home!" The uncharacteristic slang revealed her enthusiasm.

Jess had to laugh. She was beginning to catch some of her aunt's spirit.

The night before they were to leave for Scotland, Aunt Mil went to bed early. But for some reason Jess found it hard to settle down. She had made the mistake of taking out the book of poetry Graham had left for her, and it had provoked all the old longing and regret. The lines from "Ae Fond Kiss" seemed particularly poignant.

Ae fond kiss and then we sever. . . .
Never met — or never parted —
We had ne'er been broken-hearted!

That one "fond kiss" of Graham's was still a warm, vibrant memory. So were the words she had heard like an after-sound as she flung out the chapel door.

"Listen, Jess, I love you!" Graham had said fiercely.

Only afterward had those words come back to her. She had been too upset, too angry to heed them at the time. But later she remembered — when it was too late, when Graham was gone.

Finally Jess put aside Robert Burns and took up her Bible. Going over and over what had happened with Graham was an exercise in futility. They had both made mistakes. But it was over. To keep saying "if only" was self-defeating. And she was going to stop. There was no changing the past.

With that thought she turned to Philippians 3:13, found Paul's admonition, and read it over and over, ". . . forgetting those things which are behind, and reaching forth unto those things which are before."

I will learn from this experience, Jess told herself firmly as she turned out the lamp. *But I won't let it depress me or make me bitter.*

With God's help, she added as she thumped her pillow into a ball and lay down to sleep.

The next day as Jess stood on the platform at the railroad station waiting for the porter to load their luggage into their compartment, she watched a group of men in sporting tweeds and Norfolk jackets overseeing an assortment of leather suitcases, golfing bags, shotgun cases, fishing tackle, and other assorted equipment stacked on a baggage trolley.

She could overhear the conversation about the chances of hooking a salmon or the prospects of hunting once they got to Scotland.

Irrelevantly — or was it? — the enigmatic announcement Graham had made to explain his unexpected departure from Fortnay Hall sprang into Jess's mind.

"Said he was going fishing."

Something rang a bell. Could Graham have possibly meant he was going to Scotland to fish? No place on earth was more famous for its clear streams and abundant fish than Scotland.

An irrational hope fluttered in Jess's heart, then just as quickly faded. Even if Graham was in Scotland, what were their chances of running into him? If he had gone there to fish he had probably gone to some remote fishing lodge, who could know where?

Graham had talked about going hiking, camping, fishing with his grandfather in the wilderness areas of the Sierra Nevada Mountains of California when he was a young boy. He had spoken enthusiastically about hiking the Muir Trail in Yosemite Valley.

"Grandad was a great admirer of John Muir, who as you might know was a Scotsman. He was almost singlehandedly responsible for getting President Theodore Roosevelt to establish Yosemite as a national park. In fact, John Muir is credited with being the catalyst for the whole national park system in the United States," he had told Jess.

"Another great contribution to the whole world by a Scot!" she had teased. "You do have some national pride, Graham."

He laughed. "True to the breed, I guess."

He was like her own uncles, Jess thought. Second and third generations removed from Scotland, they still liked nothing better than to put on their tartans on Robert Burns's birthday and brag about Scotland's glory. Graham was right. It was in the blood.

If Graham had been born in another century, Jess was sure he would have made a great chieftan. He certainly looked the part with his tall, broad-shouldered body, the dark red hair, the strong jaw and noble features, the almost arrogant stance.

But Jess didn't want to think about Graham any more. She turned away from the group of sportsmen and concentrated on a harried looking young woman with a whining five-year-old child tugging on her hand as she tried to instruct a porter about her luggage.

With an unconscious gesture, Jess touched the yellow silk scarf she had knotted around her throat that morning. It was a nice accent to her outfit, the pale yellow sweater and beige jacket, she told herself. But she knew the real reason she wore it so often was that it was a link with Graham she was not yet ready to give up.

Maybe some day when she got home, she would pack it away with the other souvenirs, the tourist brochures, and other memorabilia she had collected on the trip. But not yet.

Their activities in Edinburgh were a whirlwind. They had somewhere to go, something to see every minute. It was exhilarating if exhausting, and as Aunt Mil commented, "There must be something in the

Scottish air that reactivates our Scottish genes and gives us so much energy."

They both wanted to capture every nuance, keep every memory to take back home to their relatives who had never set foot on Scotland's soil.

They toured the great Edinburgh Castle, that stands like a fortress high above the city and is older than the city itself. It was the storm center of much of Scotland's turbulent history.

"Too bad you won't be here in August," their guide lamented. "That's the time of the international festival, and there are great doings here. They put floodlights on the castle wall and play the grand spectacle of the Military Tattoo out on the Esplanade. It's a great gathering of the troops and pipers."

The magnificent Cathedral Church of St. Giles was next on their list of must-see sites. Its crown spire was a well-known landmark of the city. They were awed by its splendor, the gorgeous chancel with its vivid stained-glass windows and incredible carvings and the Chapel of the Order of the Thistle, the small ornate worship place for the premier order of Scottish knights. Respectfully they viewed the statue of the famous sixteenth-century reformer, John Knox. It was said that Mary, Queen of Scots, feared his prayers more than all the world's armies.

Another statue Jess insisted on seeing in Edinburgh was that of "Greyfriars Bobby" the little dog from the beloved childhood story.

And down at Princes Street Gardens, they admired the soaring, Neo-Gothic monument to Sir Walter Scott, who had called Edinburgh "mine own romantic town" and made Scotland familiar to the world with his romantic novels.

They spent nearly a day on Canongate, walking in the restored Old Town, so quaint and picturesque. Their fourth day they shopped on Princes Street across from the beautiful gardens.

"Well, I've had my fill of sightseeing for a while!" Aunt Mil told Jess emphatically. "Now, I think we should just take our time and shop for ourselves."

The first order of the day was to buy Macdonald tartan kilts, and Aunt Mil insisted Jess get the full traditional regalia.

"But, Auntie, I don't know that I'd ever wear it!" protested Jess mildly.

"You'll have a chance, Jessamyn, I'm sure. There'll be some special occasion when it will be the only appropriate thing for a Scotswoman to wear." She nodded her head smiling confidently.

While they were picking out their skirts in their own clan plaid, Jess's gaze kept wandering over to where other material was displayed, each with the identifying clan above. Her eyes kept seeking out the Campbell tartan.

She felt like a traitor. But she was curious.

Finally laden with bundles and boxes, they went back to their hotel and dumped the day's plunder on the bed. While Aunt Mil stretched out on her bed, Jess tried on her formal attire.

"I love it! I didn't think I would, but I do!" Jess exclaimed as she modeled it for her aunt.

"It really suits you!" declared Aunt Mil. "You look like a 'bonnie lassie' for sure."

Jess pirouetted in front of the full-length mirror, surveying herself critically. *It is surprisingly becoming,* she thought.

Underneath the fitted black velvet jacket was the white silk blouse with a froth of lace at the throat and cuffs. Then the long full skirt flaunted the brilliant blues, greens, yellows, and reds of the Macdonald tartan.

As she regarded her reflection Jess had one fleeting regret. She wished Graham Campbell could see her like this.

At almost the same time she imagined how he would look in full Highland regalia.

What a figure he would cut! The colorful tartan would be draped over one shoulder and fastened with a silver brooch. The kilt and sporran, knee socks and brogues, and the Balmoral bonnet, a type of tam with a crest would complete Graham's proud display of Scots heritage.

How silly! What a dreamer you are, Jessamyn Baird! she scoffed in self-ridicule.

When are you going to wake up and realize you're never going to see Graham Campbell again — with or without a tartan?

Chapter
Fourteen

Leaning on the railing of the upper deck of the ferry to Skye, Jess felt the salt spray on her face.

She shivered slightly, buttoned the top button of her coat, turned up its collar and tightened the knot of her yellow scarf around her head. The wind was cool, but something else had sent that little tremor down her spine. Gazing out across the shimmering water, Jess herself was submerged in an eerie sensation of coming home.

Of course, she had spent hours looking at beautiful pictures of just such scenes as she now looked out over. It was probably that that made it all seem so familiar, as though she had been here before. But still, Jess had a feeling of awe at the strong inner knowing.

Before they had left for Skye, Jess had steeped herself in its history. She had been particularly interested in reading about the gallant Flora Macdonald, heroine of the cause of the fabled Bonnie Prince Charlie in his quest for the British throne.

Since Aunt Mil had told her their family could trace their heritage from this illustrious woman, Jess had been eager to find out more about her kinswoman. Jess was surprised to learn that at the time of her daring plan to rescue the prince, Flora had only been twenty-three, Jess's own age.

Skye itself was most closely associated with the clan of Macdonald. Perhaps that is why she felt this intrinsic bond as the ferry boat moved toward the most legendary of the Western Islands.

Even the air had a difference, a strange sharpness, she mused as she inhaled deeply. It was more than just the tanginess of the sea. It was unlike anything she had ever breathed before.

Oh, Jess, she reprimanded herself. *You are so imaginative!*

"You have the eyes of a dreamer." That comment Graham had made about her the first time they talked rang in Jess's ears. *He had seen it and said it even before he had come to know her,* she thought. It was as if he saw and recognized what few others knew, at least not until they knew her longer.

An involuntary shudder made Jess draw

her coat collar closer and decide to go down to the lounge to get out of the wind for a while, get a warm cup of tea, and stop these foolish imaginings.

Below deck, in the comfortably warm salon, Jess found Aunt Mil in a spritely conversation with a couple. The ruddy-cheeked, rusty-haired man wore a tweed jacket and kilt. Seeing Jess, Aunt Mil beckoned her over to join them. "My niece, Jessamyn Baird, the Macleods," she introduced.

"Mr. and Mrs. Macleod are also of the Clanranald." Aunt Mil told Jess. "They're going to visit relatives on Skye mainly because there's going to be a clan gathering, a sort of family reunion of all the different clans who trace their heritage to that origin."

"And certainly the Macdonalds would be welcome," Mr. Macleod said heartily. "On the island of Skye the name Macdonald is a badge of glory."

Jess, who had bought a book in Edinburgh about the Scottish clans, listened as the animated discussion went on among the three others. Amazingly the feeling of kinship among the related clans was very strong still, almost as strong as long ago when Scotland was a place of violent feuding.

Jess had been made aware of how deep

this feeling went when she and Aunt Mil traveled to Glencoe, site of the tragic massacre of the Macdonald clan by the Campbells.

After their defeat by the English, the clans who had supported James as the heir to the Scottish throne were promised pardon on the understanding that they would pledge allegiance to King William by January 1, 1692. The Macdonalds, unfortunately, arrived late and the English authorities decided to make an example of these "wild Highlanders." They engaged the Campbells in a conspiracy. The Campbells, long-time enemies of the Macdonalds in the clan feuds, made the journey to Glencoe and accepted the hospitality of their ancient foe for two weeks before they turned around and murdered them. The book said that in Gaelic, Glencoe is known as "the glen of weeping, weeping for fathers and brothers treacherously slain." A footnote sent a pang through Jess's heart. "In some places in the Highlands the name Campbell is equivalent to 'betrayal.'"

Their guide had lamented, "If it had been done in an open fight, it would not have been thought so treacherous. But to kill a man in his bed —" He had shaken his head sadly. "It was an affront to the tradition of Highland hospitality."

Poor Graham, Jess had thought with a certain melancholy. But then, she remembered, as he had reminded her, he was also kin to — in fact, named after — the "gallant Grahams," famous Scottish heroes. "Every family, every clan for that matter, has some black sheep, some skeletons in the closet," he had said ruefully.

There was a recognizable slowing down of the motion of the boat, and the constant sound of the engines had slowed to a persistent hum. Mr. Macleod became alert,

"We're coming into the harbor now," he announced.

Jess put on her coat and gathered up her scarf.

"I think I'll go up on deck again," she said. "Nice to have met you." She nodded to the Macleods.

"Oh, we'll meet again, lass," Mr. Macleod assured her jovially. "At the clan gathering, for sure!"

"Your aunt's said you'll both be there," agreed Mrs. Macleod with a twinkle in her clear blue eyes.

"Well, then, I suppose I will!" Jess laughed.

She climbed the stairway back to the deck

and took a place at the rail as the ferry slowly moved in to a wooden dock.

The sound of the ferry's horns announcing its arrival mingled with the harsh cries of seagulls swooping overhead. Jess caught glimpses of rough stone buildings, whitewashed and red-trimmed, set against picture-postcard blue skies. Once again she felt a little thrill of homecoming.

The minute she walked down the gangplank Jess felt the magic. It almost overwhelmed her, and she found herself quite choked with emotion. While Aunt Mil was busy seeing to their luggage, giving the cab driver the address of the bed and breakfast where they had reservations, Jess seemed unable to move or speak.

The atmosphere of the islands was overpowering. The mystical light cast by the late afternoon sun spoke to her innermost spirit.

The mystifying, awe-inspiring spell was immediately dismissed by the briskly cheerful, bustling personality of their B & B hostess Sara MacDougall who greeted them at the front door. Her flaming red hair intensified this impression of her personality. She immediately told Aunt Mil that they were kinswomen in view of the fact that Sara had been a Macleod before her marriage and MacDougall was one of the smaller clans encompassed by the big Clanranald to which the three others, Macdonald, Macleod and MacDougall, all belonged!

She ushered them right into the parlor to have their tea. Jess had discovered it was always tea time in Scotland no matter what the time of day.

This tea, a hearty one, was served to them before a welcoming fire in front of a fireplace. Over it hung a familiar handsome painting of a Highland stag. Mrs. MacDougall's conversation never missed a beat as she piled their plates high with scones, bread and butter, slivers of ham, two kinds of jam, and large slices of a lemony seed cake.

If Jess had had an idea that Scots were not talkative, Mrs. MacDougall quickly put that to rest. She wanted to hear all about their travels and wanted to tell them all about Skye.

"It's like no other place on earth," she said emphatically with a positive nod. "Many another place has its own legends and tales, but we have more and better! And you'll be sure to be staying for the grand clan gathering then, won't you?" she asked.

"Indeed, yes!" rejoined Aunt Mil.

"Oh, we'll be having a fine time then!" Mrs. MacDougall assured her.

She was interrupted by a pretty girl, with cheeks like rosy winter apples and flamboyant red hair.

"Oh, here's Fiona, my niece and my helper," she introduced her. "She'll show you to your rooms now if you've had enough to stave you off till supper."

Jess avoided glancing at Aunt Mil. She devoutly hoped supper was a long time off as she had helped herself generously to the wonderful tea.

Jess's room, adjoining Aunt Mil's, was charming with cheerful flowered chintz and a polished brass bed boasting a handmade coverlet and ruffled pillows.

Jess looked out the window and saw that a light rain was falling. Scottish weather, she had discovered, was unpredictable. All sunshine, pastel skies, one hour, and low clouds and stormy, the next. There had been no two days alike in their entire stay in Scotland.

Somehow the weather had seemed to reflect her moods — some days glowing with newfound joy, others somber with vague unhappiness. She knew her regrets about Graham had turned her into an emotional weather vane.

When she could forget even for a few hours, she was fine. Why had a man she had known for such a brief time left such a pervasive void in her life?

What I need is a rainbow, Jess thought. Her Grandmother Jeanie used to tell her a rainbow was God's promise. No matter how dark life seemed, after the storm was over, the beautiful arc of colors would appear, bringing new hope.

Well, she would keep looking for a rainbow and just learn to cope with the loss of Graham Campbell. She would have to.

Those first few days on Skye, Jess often wished she were an artist. From her first glimpse, Skye had taken hold of Jess — captured her in its spell. Every romantic instinct in her responded to the island's special mystical atmosphere.

It was so beautiful, so unique, she would have liked to have the skill to paint it. As it was, every morning after they came, Jess spent hours walking.

The island was small and everywhere she walked she was within moments of a glimpse of the sea. Often she walked down to watch the fishermen mending nets or working on their boats, for fishing was the main occupation of the islanders. Then she would climb past the gray stone cottages along the shore, where rosy-cheeked children paused to watch her pass and wave to her. She breathed deeply of the soft, sweet air with its tinge of salt spray and kelp. She loved the walks best, perhaps, on the high, windy slopes, amid the yellow clumps of gorse and purple heather.

There her spirit seemed to soar. It was there that Jess first heard the music of the bagpipes echoing up through the strath, or valley. In the open air the pipes had a mystical quality. The plaintive sound stirred something deep inside Jess, its strange cacophony of notes bringing an inner exultation.

Once on the way back to Mrs. MacDougall's she paused on a steep hillside overlooking a clear, rushing stream and saw a lone fisherman casting his rod from a rock.

For one heart-clutching moment Jess thought it might be Graham. There had been something poignantly familiar about the way he had moved, the sureness of his casting arm, the breadth of shoulders and shape of head. But the resemblance was fleeting, for as the thought surfaced the man turned, as if drawn by her staring, and looked up at her. She saw, of course, that it was not Graham.

Walking on, Jessamyn couldn't help thinking about him. Was he somewhere in Scotland fishing some crystal stream? And if he was, did he ever think of her?

Foolish thoughts, empty dreams, she admonished herself, lifting her head and walking faster. *Forget Graham Campbell,* she commanded her wayward heart.

She made the commitment in vain. Everything about Scotland, even about Skye, reminded her of him.

One day she and Aunt Mil drove over to Dunvegan Castle. Once only accessible by sea, the castle was the hereditary stronghold of the Clan Macleod. According to Aunt Mil's informants on the ferry, they still held their Parliament there. The rocky fortress, built to withstand savage attacks, was a brooding reminder of Scotland's clan wars.

The weekend brought the first day of the clan gathering which would be opened by a ceremonial banquet and party.

At breakfast that morning Mrs. MacDougall regaled Jess with an account of the fun and festivities in store for her that evening. "Oh, you've never seen such dancing!" Mrs. MacDougall shook her head. "I think our own dancers and pipers are as good as any you'd see at the international festival in Edinburgh in August," she declared as she urged Jess to take another warm "bap" fresh from the oven.

It took some will power to resist it, but

since Jess had already eaten a typical Highland breakfast of porridge, bacon, eggs, and baps, the floury soft rolls Mrs. Mac-Dougall made fresh each morning, she managed to do it.

"But you need your energy if you're going walking again this morning," Mrs. MacDougall persisted.

Jess shook her head and rose from the table. "I won't be able to walk a step if I do, Mrs. MacDougall! Thank you just the same," Jess replied, smiling to take any sting of rejection from her refusal.

In contrast to the excited anticipation of everyone else around the MacDougall household, Jess felt an intangible melancholy. She thought it best to remove herself from the busy preparations for the evening's gaiety by taking an extra long morning walk. But that evening even Jess found herself responding to the excitement and anticipation around her.

When the first high, sharp skirl of pipes pierced the crystalline night air, Jess felt a peculiar excitement. As she and Aunt Mil walked to the hall of the clan gathering, the shrill tones had a double effect. Running along her scalp and down her spine was a mixed nerve-rending yet thrilling response.

The wailing sound climbed into a reedy, sustained note. When they entered the hall, its walls seemed to resound triumphantly with the rich traditional melody of the Highland pipers. Jess felt herself immediately caught up in the joyous occasion.

All the clans who claimed kinship with Clanranald were assembled, the bright colors of their plaid tartans distinguishing one from the other. Jess had learned that in the days of the fierce inter-clan fights, the chieftan needed to recognize which warriors were his by sight. Thus emerged the unique colors and patterns of each tartan.

Everyone at the gathering seemed to recognize and know the tartans at a glance. Jess and Aunt Mil were immediately greeted, welcomed, and surrounded by their clansmen. Shown to one of the tables on the edge of the big dance floor, they were seated just in time for the exhibition dances to begin.

The first was the famous sword dance, skillfully performed by a group of eight young men. All were traditionally costumed with kilts, tartans, and Glengarry caps. The narrow hats were shaped like upturned rowboats and trimmed with short ribbons in the back. As the music began, the dancers started the intricate steps over the crossed swords placed on the floor. They were all big, brawny fellows, but their steps were as light, quick, and precise as any ballerina's. The dance ended to wildly enthusiastic applause.

As the applause faded, the music for the popular country reel started up, and immediately Jess was claimed by a tall, smiling kinsman who introduced himself as Logan and who, she learned later, was Mrs. MacDougall's nephew.

Highland dances were very spritely and vigorous, Jess soon discovered. By the end of the reel she was breathless. Logan went to get her some refreshing punch and Jess gratefully watched the next reel. Some of the dancers, however, were apparently inexhaustible. They moved effortlessly through reel after reel.

Finally there was a sort of intermission. The dancers, ready at last for rest and refreshment, left the dance floor to a group of male singers. In kilt and tartan of the Dress Macdonald they sang without accompaniment. Mrs. MacDougall informed Jess in a stage-whisper that their song was said to have been composed by Flora Macdonald herself.

As the strong, rich voices rose Jess listened

to the words, feeling a thrill of pride in her own Scottish heritage.

Ye'll hear of the chieftains of old
Those sons of valour and worth.
But Charlie's own favorite clan was
Macdonald, the pride of the north.

Oh, hie to the Highlands, my laddie!
Be welcomed by hearts warm and true,
But there's where ye'll see my ain laddie,
The tartans and bonnets of blue.

This song was applauded with such great enthusiasm that the crowd rose to a standing ovation and cheered. Then there was a general flowing back onto the dance floor, as the band struck up a tune that seemed familiar to all. The dancers took their places in facing rows all singing "You're welcome, Charlie Stuart." There could be no doubt in anyone's mind where this group of Highlanders stood in relation to "Bonnie Prince Charlie," Jess concluded.

The music quickened, and the dancers began a prancing step to its beat, moving forward in groups of three, wheeling in semicircles, and performing a variety of complex formations, then moving in rapid, intrepid, and perfect timing back to their original positions. The people around the room clapped the rhythm faster and faster until the music, the dancing, and the clapping all ended in a happy burst of laughter and merriment.

At midnight a fabulous feast was set out on long tables in a room adjoining the ballroom. Incredibly Jess was hungry, something she had not expected to be after Mrs. MacDougall's plenteous and hearty supper. But the ladies of Skye and the Clanranald had outdone themselves. A grand spread of food displayed salmon in many forms from baked to mousse, salads and breads of every kind, and cakes and pies. Of course, there was also a typical Scots dessert of creamy pudding laced with the bittersweet marmalade Scotland is famous for. This was accompanied by black bun, dark, rich currant fruitcake in a pastry shell.

After sampling everything, Jess didn't think she could move again. But soon the likable Logan was back, asking her to be his partner for another dance. When she demurred, he persuaded, "Oh, this is not a reel! It's a strathspey and it's much slower, more sedate," he assured her.

He was so persuasive she could not refuse and soon found herself again on the dance floor. Logan was a fine dancer leading her easily through the steps, and when the music ended, Jess felt she could accept another round.

When at last the band began to play "Auld Lang Syne" and each group rose around the table and clasped hands to sing, Jess had a nostalgic, heartstopping moment.

Across the room she saw the back of a tall man at another table. His dark red hair glowed under the lights like polished mahogany. He was in formal dress, broad-shouldered under the black velvet jacket. It was only a split-second reaction. Then Jess realized, of course, it wasn't possible. What would Graham *Campbell* be doing at a *Macdonald* clan gathering?

Walking back to the B & B Jess was pensive. After the fun and gaiety of the evening she felt a curious letdown. The moon was cradled in silver clouds that seemed to rock gently above the treetops as the wind moved them back and forth, and Jess's heart felt tight with longing. Something tugged at her heartstrings. Perhaps it was the knowledge that in another day they would be leaving Skye, leaving Scotland.

"Farewell, lovely Skye — isle of the valiant, the brave, the free. Blow the wind o'er the bonny, blue sea, Bring my true love, safely to me." The words of one of those lovely Celtic legends put to music whispered softly in Jess's mind.

But Jess knew nothing would bring her own true love back to her.

Chapter
Fifteen

Jess was not at all sure she was in the proper spirit to go to church that Sunday morning. But she decided that in John Calvin's Scotland, feelings certainly should be put aside. Probably the fact that she did not feel like going meant she needed to go.

Aunt Mil had come down with a cold and decided to stay in bed and nurse it. So Jess donned her raincoat and scarf and set out alone along the quiet village streets to the small stone church.

The rain of the night before had gradually stopped, and here and there patches of blue peeped between the shredding gray cotton clouds. A glorious morning was promised as sunlight tinted the gauzy mist lifting from the distant hills in lavender and blue.

Once she was inside the raftered interior of the little "kirk" its familiarity struck Jess at once, and she felt at peace. It was not unlike her childhood church in her hometown. When she saw the carved quotation from Hebrews 13:8 on one of the beams, "Jesus Christ the same yesterday, today and forever," she felt comfortingly at home.

Only a handful of people made up the congregation but their voices were strong and true as they sang the familiar hymns. The sermon, given by a young, sandy-haired minister in the lilting burr Jess had come to love, was uplifting.

At the closing hymn, Jess's ear picked up the words of the favorite psalm of praise, sung a little differently from what she was used to — "I to the hills will lift mine eyes,/From whence doth come mine aid" — but all the same it had never seemed more appropriate than here in this small Highland church where every window offered a glimpse of the iridescent hills.

Light of heart and at peace with herself and the world after the service, Jess decided to walk a little farther before going back to Mrs. MacDougall's. The fresh clear air almost sparkled, and Jess drew in long breaths as she walked past the edge of the village into the countryside. Everywhere the fields and hills were patchwork colors of gold and purple, for the rains had coaxed out the blossoms. The hillsides were carpeted with lovely lavender heather.

Not fully aware of how far she had come, Jess continued climbing until she reached the top of a hillock and suddenly there was the sea. The sky stretched above it — an endless bright canopy of blue over the shining silvered jade of the water. It was so beautiful that Jess felt a rush of happiness.

The wind from the sea tossed her hair forward over her face. Brushing it back with one hand, she groped with the other for her scarf to tie it back and discovered it was gone. Automatically she searched both raincoat pockets, but it wasn't in either one. She must have dropped it somewhere along the way.

Jess felt a pang of dismay. It wasn't so much the scarf itself that distressed her as its emotional associations.

Sighing, she started walking on. Suddenly she thought she heard her name called. She halted for a minute, then walked on, thinking it must have been a trick of the wind moving along the edge of the cliff. Then it came again, louder this time, clearer.

"Jessamyn! Jess!"

She whirled around and stood still in shocked surprise.

Graham! The sun on the top of that burnished thatch of hair turned it into a glow-

248

ing russet. His wide shoulders were hunched against the wind in the flapping tan raincoat, its belt flying behind. Graham striding toward her. *Graham — here in Skye!*

Jess's heart began pounding. She stood motionless, watching him approach. He was beaming and saying her name over and over! His long strides bridged the space between them, until he stood towering over her.

Her hair was damp with mist and curling around her face and forehead. She put up one trembling hand to push the flying curls back when Graham took her yellow scarf from his raincoat pocket and held it out.

"You dropped this," he told her gently. Then folding it into a neat triangle, he put it around her head and awkwardly tied it under her chin. After that, he held her face in both his hands and simply looked at her for a long moment.

"Where did you find it?" she whispered.

"At the 'wee kirk' down there," he replied. A slight smile touched his mouth. "I still believe what my Scottish grandmother told me — 'You find the nicest girls in church.'"

"But what are you doing here — in Skye?" Jess stammered.

Graham grinned.

"Happenstance? Fate?" He paused. "Actually I came to Scotland for the fishing.

My grandad taught me to fish when I was a kid. I couldn't go back to the States and tell him I hadn't tried the world-famous streams of Scotland for salmon. So I came, and then a Scotsman I met told me I had to come to Skye. So I did." He paused again, and a mischievous glint suddenly lit his blue eyes.

"I'm told I just missed a Highlander high fling — the gathering of the clan. Probably a good thing . . . I'm not sure I'd have been all that welcome."

Here he paused once more, this time for a long moment. Then he asked gently, "Am I welcome with you, Jess? Or are you still angry with me?"

Not waiting for her to answer, Graham rushed on. "I know I was wrong to blurt out all the things I said about Peter — about the Fortnays. And I should probably have stayed and tried to make peace with you before I left Fortnay Hall, but I thought I'd caused enough damage. I decided to leave a clear field for Peter, if that was what you wanted."

Jess did not say anything. She just kept looking up at Graham, bewildered by his flow of words.

"I'm not sure now that I'm not wrong again. But I decided to take the risk anyway. I have to take the chance even if it's only one in a million.

"When I learned you and your aunt were staying here in Skye, I argued with myself for hours. I walked miles, trying to talk myself out of coming to tell you how I felt. I thought I'd already bungled things too badly . . . and that you were probably in love with someone else . . ."

Graham's voice was low and even with a fierce intensity as he asked, "Jess, are you in love with Peter?"

Now, Graham's hands moved to her shoulders. She could feel his fingers gripping them, holding her quite still so she could not turn away.

Dazedly Jess shook her head.

Was this really happening? Was it true that Graham was here, appearing out of the mist like an answer to her dreams, hopes, and prayers?

"No, Graham, there's no one else, and I'm not in love with Peter Fortnay. I never was," she replied.

A smile broke out on Graham's face, relief followed quickly by joy.

"You mean that, Jess?" he demanded.

"Of course!"

"Then, is there . . ." He hesitated. "Is there a chance for *me?*"

Jess looked at him uncertainly. Then she saw the anxiety in his eyes, and wildly sweet tenderness for him swept over her.

She wanted to reach up and touch that thick thatch of russet hair and — yes, to kiss that deceptively stern mouth and see him smile.

"Well?" he frowned anxiously, giving her a little shake.

Jess still could not find words. Was this a romantic dream? Or was it really happening?

"Jess, answer me —" Graham pleaded. "Maybe, you think I'm too old for you —" he suggested hesitantly. "I *am* thirty-five."

"Oh, no!" Jess exclaimed. "Just right! *Exactly right!*" They started laughing together, and he hugged her to him.

"Oh, darling Jess, for a minute there you had me going!" he said, but there was a note of triumph in his voice. "I was prepared for a turndown."

"But I thought —" Jess began, but she never got to finish her sentence, for Graham bent down and lifted her chin. Their lips met in a kiss so sweet and so natural they might have had quite a lot of practice.

When after a long while Jess opened her eyes and looked into Graham's, there was a hint of a laughter there.

"There's so much to say, so many questions," she murmured as she reached up to ruffle his already unruly hair.

"There'll be plenty of time to ask them . . . and to answer them," Graham said. "I've got quite a few of my own. I can't quite believe you're here in my arms, that I'm holding you, that I actually had the courage — Well, 'Faint heart ne'er won fair lady,' right? Hey! Now that's an old-fashioned, *romantic* thing to say!" Graham laughed. "I can't believe *I* said it!"

Graham held Jess out at arm's length for a minute and sternly asked, "What actually happened between you and Peter? When I left Fortnay Hall I was convinced that my own stupidity had practically thrown you into Lord Peter's waiting arms."

"Well, as far as I know, his engagement to Hilary Holmes is back on, and they'll probably marry and live happily ever after — just like in all the good fairy tales!" Jess told him teasingly.

Then more seriously she said, "Graham, you were wrong about Peter and me. He was never seriously interested. Oh, attracted, maybe, as I was, and flattered a little. The truth is —" and Jess tilted her head to one side and glanced up at Graham with a teasing smile, "I think I was having a love affair with England!" She paused, then added mischievously, "But then I hadn't seen *Scotland!*"

All around them swirled the Scottish mist. Graham leaned forward and kissed her lips, the dimple to one side of it, the tip of her nose. Brushing back her mist-diamonded hair, he kissed her mouth again. His mouth was warm and insistent. His arms tightened in an embrace she had longed for but not dared to hope would ever happen.

Her arms moved to his shoulders. Her hands clasped around his neck. He drew her close, and time and space seemed to merge into a spinning circle in which only they two existed. With a blinding reality, Jess knew that she had never felt so loved, so safe, so cherished as here in Graham's embrace.

At last, his lips moved against her cheek, whispering, "Come on, we're getting soaked out here." Like a chameleon the Scottish weather had changed suddenly, and a fine soft rain was falling. Arms around each other, they started down the hill together.

As they made their way along the steep path twisting down through the lichen-covered rocks, Graham suddenly halted. Stooping down, he plucked something, then turned and handed it to her with a shy smile.

"A sprig of *white* heather!" he announced with something like awe. "You know it's very rare. Most heather is purple, and to find white heather is considered 'vera lucky indeed.' A Scottish bride carries a tiny sprig in the bridal bouquet to symbolize hope of a long and happy marriage."

Not romantic? This man? Jess smiled to herself as she tucked the sprig of heather into her coat lapel, then put her arm through Graham's again.

"Incidentally, did I tell you that northern California, where I live, is the only place outside Scotland where heather grows naturally?" he asked, as they started walking again.

Looking up at her tall companion, Jess thought blissfully, *Here is everything I have ever wanted in a man — someone to love me, to share my faith and life.* Here was her promised rainbow, the heart's desire her grandmother had told her to trust the Lord for, the fulfillment of all her dreams.

White heather or no white heather, Jess considered herself very lucky indeed!

At Mrs. MacDougall's they found tea waiting and a glowing fire in the fireplace of the small sitting room. The bright-eyed, canny Scotswoman, a devotee of "soaps" and love stories, knew a real romance when she saw one. She tiptoed out leaving them to themselves.

Sitting in the firelight with Graham,

drinking hot tea, Jess sighed, treasuring this nearly perfect moment. She knew there would never be another quite like it.

But if prayers are answered and dreams come true, some day in their own home on a California hillside overlooking the sea they might be listening to the sound of the drumming surf and the skirling wind — a wind ever fragrant with the scent of heather.